THE SOUND
OF ANGELS

THE SOUND OF ANGELS

LISA SILVERTHORNE

WILDSIDE PRESS

CONTENTS

DEEP WATERS
DEAN WESLEY SMITH

For a number of months now, I've tried to figure out exactly when Lisa Silverthorne came into my consciousness as a writer of wonderful, powerful stories. I haven't been able to figure it out, to be honest. It just seems like she's always been there in one form or another, either in my reading of anthologies, or my editing of magazines.

And yet, Lisa isn't that old, hasn't really been around that long, at least not compared to my time in this fabled land of publishing. In reality, as it is with many writers, after years of work, she is just now starting to really catch the editors' and publishers' eyes regularly with her stories. Or, for lack of a better way of putting it, she's just getting the wind in the sails of her career.

This book is a great place to start your reading of her work.

So why am I writing this introduction? I never do these things, ever, for anyone. Yet here I sit, gladly writing this one. Why?

Because she asked me, and I felt honored, to be honest. I've been a fan of her work, and her as a person, so it just didn't dawn on me to say no. Plus, I wanted to read the book.

Lisa has also been a welcome guest here in my home a number of times over the past few years. Actually, she's here now, as I finish reading this collection full of powerful stories. She's been working with Gardner Dozois and my, Kristine Kathryn Rusch, to make her future stories even better. That desire to learn and keep getting better is one of the many things I love about Lisa. (She's also one of the nicest people you're ever going to meet, but don't tell her I said so. It will screw up my reputation as a grumpy old guy.)

So, for this week, she's been here working and writing more stories and I've been reading her collection. It's been a busy week. I'm tired, stressed from having guests here, and under deadline for a book of my own. Yet Lisa's stories kept me reading, every one of them, which is unusual for me with any writer. Those who know me, know I don't say things like that lightly. I have no problem telling someone, great friends even, that I couldn't get past page two of their story.

All of Lisa's stories in this book kept me reading and enjoying the language, the stories, the emotions. Let me repeat that. All of them.

It's also interesting to me that Lisa picked the title of the story "The Sound of Angels" for the title of this book. A perfect pick, in my opinion. It's a story that in a very few number of words shows many of Lisa's strengths as a writer. The story, even though science fiction based, is very human focused, dealing with love and loss and relationships and ties that hold us all to one another. Great science fiction.

Perfect Lisa Silverthorne.

But please, don't just stop with the title story. Work your way through this book like you would a wonderful bottle of wine with a many course meal, savoring the different flavors and textures that Lisa brings to her work with amazing grace and style and skill. You will find yourself very pleased when you finish, and I'm sure you will start looking for more Lisa Silverthorne stories as they appear in magazines and anthologies, her own books. And trust me, I know her, there will be many more. She has just started to tap her very deep waters of talent.

But for the moment, settle back with this wonderful sampler into the worlds and characters and emotions of Lisa Silverthorne. You'll be glad you did. I sure was.

WHEN SPARROWS FALL

It begins with a chill wind and screams. Burnt scent of jet fuel and whistle of air across torn wings. I toss in my bed, desperately wanting it to be a dream, and flail against the terrified voices, the hush of descent. There is a horrible, rushing sound in my ears. At the whisper of death and the gouging of metal against ground, I bolt up from the bed, my skin clammy with sweat. My stomach aches and tears gather in my eyes. Please—not another one.

Turning on the light, I sit up and hug my pillow. Icy fear trembles through my body and my teeth chatter. I rock against the head-board, trying to dislodge the images. My hands hurt. I glance down at them. They're burnt and smell of jet fuel. My hands haven't burned in a long time. It's a bad crash—a jet. Lots of people.

Sunrise is a couple of hours off and he'll be calling. Maybe by then I can pull myself together?

In a short while, my shaking stops, the blankets at last warming me. I rise slowly and go into the kitchen to make some coffee. After two cups, I slip into the shower and dress. The horizon is fiery now. I pour myself another cup of coffee and wait.

Finally, I lay my hand against the phone and a heartbeat later, it rings. My trembling returns.

"Hello, Mark," I say, my voice raspy.

"Uh—Stacia?" NTSB Investigator Mark Vincent's voice shakes more than usual this time.

"It's a jet, isn't it?" I ask, my hands still throbbing.

A long sigh hisses through the receiver. "Yes, Stace. Two hundred people dead. Only one survivor. We're still looking for the black box."

My heart twists at the ghostly feel of a stuffed bear and the image of a little girl clutching it like a life preserver, her head down. The whistle of air across the plane's fuselage echoes in the phone's static. The impact is sharp then numbing. I lurch forward. The silence is heavy. They always call me when the black box is lost.

I glance out the window at the darkness beginning to lighten on the horizon and I hear the fragile chirp of birds. Morning will come soon.

They say that God hears even a sparrow when it falls to the ground. What must He hear when two hundred of his own fall?

"I'll be there in four hours," I say finally, my voice still hoarse.

"But I didn't tell you where the crash site is."

I sigh. I've been working with NTSB investigators for almost a year now, yet Mark hasn't gotten used to what I see.

"I know where it is," I say calmly. "An old growth forest northwest of me." I can smell the tang of pine nettles and the raw stench of fire. And I see the blackened furrows and broken trees, the long, white plane a greenstick fracture poking through the earth's brown skin.

"We can't find the box and the little girl's critical. The tower thinks it was pilot error. What went wrong?"

I clutch the receiver. "We'll know soon enough," I say and hang up the phone.

The morning coolness mists the fir trees and frames the highway. It swirls ominously across the twisty road that winds through the ancient forest toward the crash site. The heater huffs low, softening the drone of the radio that fills the silence with distraction.

Finally, I reach a roadblock where police cars huddle in the road. The grim-faced officers move almost mechanically in their rain ponchos. A policeman steps toward my car and I roll down the window. He is bleary-eyed from a sleepless night.

"I'm Stacia Evans," I tell him and offer my driver's license. "Investigator Vincent sent for me."

"Yeah, he's expecting you," says the policeman and hands back my license. His gaze falls to the gloves on my hands. "Pull your car off the road over there." He motions toward a small clearing. "You'll have to walk up to the site."

After parking my car, I start up the hillside, bracing myself as I crest the hill and stop.

Torn suitcases and mangled seat cushions, foam and springs erupting, litter the forest floor. Airplane panels lie shattered like egg shells, stark against the nettles and moss blanketing the autumn ground. Bits of fabric and seat belts cling to fir tree branches. Empty plane seats twist around tree trunks and crumple against blackened ground. I suck in a breath, but it hangs in my throat at the rows of yellow body bags lining the horizon. Slowly, I move deeper into the crash debris. At my feet is a torn, sooty tennis shoe. Just one.

Stale smoke scent is cold in the gray drizzle that has started early today. A crane squeaks nearby, loading hunks of gutted plane onto a flatbed truck. One chugs past me and lurches down the hill. I fight the urge to reach down and pick up the lone shoe. Not yet. Not until I've seen everything.

Yellow hazard suits weave through the old forest, investigators combing wreckage for clues—and the black box. A sandy-haired man, looking all of his thirty-five years, moves through the damp forest toward me.

"Stacia," he calls. "Glad you're here."

Mark Vincent's angular chin is stubbled and smudged with dirt, his blue eyes dull. His rain-dappled hazard suit creaks as he extends his hand. I hesitate then shake his hand quickly, trying to avoid images that will haunt me for weeks. They always do.

I nod toward the investigators and cleanup crews. "Have they recovered the bodies?"

"What's left of all two hundred." He glances at the crane raising one of the engines onto another flatbed. "When will you want to start?"

The hazy image of an old woman slips up from a section of

crushed seats. Her steely hair is swept back in harsh curls that reveal deep wrinkles furrowing her brow and cheeks. Her blue pantsuit is spattered with blood and dirt as she flits between workers. She reaches out to them, her misty face a mask of confusion, but they just walk past. Behind her, a young man in a torn rugby shirt and jeans crouches. He stares blankly at ruptured plane panels and luggage strewn everywhere.

A child rushes toward her mother and falls into a ghostly embrace.

The pilot walks grimly behind the investigators and surveys the damage. He grips the arm of his younger copilot, shaking his head and rubbing his eyes.

One by one, the passengers find each other and many go on, disappearing into the woods until I stand alone in the debris.

I watch them all as they search. They cling to together while the last broken remnants of their lives are swept away, leaving them only this drizzly hillside—and each other.

Even ghosts collect their dead.

"Stacia?"

A hand waves in front of my eyes and I glance up. Mark steps closer, concern on his face.

"You look like you're about to pass out." He steers me toward a pickup truck where I climb onto the open tailgate and let my muddy boots dangle. Mark slides a warm cup of coffee into my gloved hands.

He stares out at the debris. "You never get used to seeing things like this."

I shake my head and watch two hundred ghosts slipping in and out of the wreckage and I nod.

Now, a woman in a denim dress stands at the center of the wreckage, her gaze encompassing the forest and debris. In her eyes, I see panic. She calls out, but the sounds are lost in the whir of the crane, the buzz of trucks. Finally, her gaze falls to me. The graying, stuffed bear dangling from her hand makes me realize why she waits. I sigh.

"They're all so lost," I mumble, mostly to myself.

"Yeah," says Mark, "two hundred of them lost."

"I meant after the crash. It's not quite over for them yet. Not until they're finished here. It's important to them."

He stares uncertainly at me. I know he tries to see what I see. He never knows what to make of it, but he believes me. He stares at the broken plane and I know he sees nothing beyond the hazard suits and the drizzle.

"What do you mean—important?" he asks.

Sometimes, it really doesn't make any sense. Why some people survive and others die. I remember a cold autumn morning so painfully close to this one. The spray of hot jet fuel burning my flesh, the choking billows of black smoke smothering the dark compartment. I gasp, shoving that bit of broken memory away from me. It's a place I haven't gone in a long while, but the specter remains, cold and dark inside me. Like this gift of mine.

"How's the little girl?" I ask, changing the subject.

"Weaker. Still hasn't regained consciousness."

I rise from the truck and set down my cup. Then I move into the heart of the crash.

I wander with the ghosts through the rubble until the investigators and crew thin out. There is a closeness about these souls. They gather together, helping each other. At times, I feel like an intruder, but they accept my presence because I accept theirs.

I move toward the body bags and piles of luggage that have been moved back. Bending down, I pick up a black purse and that lone shoe. I run my hands across the purse and my eyes well with tears. Twenty-two C and D. An elderly couple. Toward the wing, they'd insisted the travel agent seat them there. It's safest over the wing. Inside the purse are the boarding passes. I run my finger over them, catching wisps of excitement and exhaustion—twinges of apprehension at so much money spent to fly. The shoe belongs to a 50-year-old account executive in 2A who just had a surprise birthday party and was returning home.

When I glance up, the elderly couple stands before me, bewildered and shaking their heads. The account executive stands beside them, his other tennis shoe clean and white. I reach out to them. I can't touch them, but they understand my gesture.

"Tell me, please," I say. "What happened?"

"It was so fast," says the elderly man, his voice thin and tight. His ruddy, hooked nose flattens as he talks. "One of the engines on the right side caught fire. The other one just stopped."

"The flight attendants told us to put our heads down and we just prayed," says the woman. "Now, we're here. Why?"

I shake my head. I have no answers for her.

The account executive shoulders past the older man. "The lights went out. Then a flight attendant whispered that one of the engines had stopped working." His gaze falls to the shoe I hold.

The woman's husband takes her hand. She turns toward him. Gently, the elderly man lays a hand against the account executive's sleeve and the younger man nods. Together, they walk out of the wreckage and disappear into the forest.

I see the pilot and move toward him. The investigators watch me as if I'm insane. Ignoring them, I drop down beside the pilot.

"Captain? Can you tell me what happened?"

"Engine failure." His voice is gravely and low, the pain thick in his words. "One of them ignited. The extinguishing systems didn't kick in either. Then we suffered a massive power loss and everything went off-line." He points somewhere in the distance. "I tried to land her in the clearing over that ridge, but we dropped too fast." He shakes his head, his ghost fingers gripping his brown hair. "Some of us might have made it. What have I done?"

I lay my hand against the air where his shoulder would have been. "Your best. Captain, you had no engines. You were over mountains and forest. You did your best. But the tower suspects pilot error. That's why I'm here. You've got to help me find the black box, Captain."

His lined face lifts toward me. "They can't find it?"

I shake my head.

"And they think it's my fault?"

"Not if we can find the black box. Can you help?"

"I'll call my crew together," he says urgently, rising from the ground. Having a purpose stirs him to action. "We'll find it." He flits toward his crewmembers, but stops and turns to me again. "How long do we have?"

I smile. "As long as it takes."

Soon, I'm alone in the debris again. I pace the rows of body bags that are being loaded into trucks. Shortly, the bodies will be carried away to next-of-kin. I reach down and touch a few of the bags, 14B, 6A, 26A—Seattle, Buffalo, Phoenix. So many stories, so many places . . . so many ripples. They play behind my eyes, a grand-daughter going to her grandparents' fiftieth anniversary, a couple on vacation, a woman going to a wedding. I see their stories as if they are my own and it chokes me up. I inhale sharply and continue to pace.

I glance toward the trees and realize I'm not alone. The woman in denim still waits. Ten years fold back like the ragged plane panels at my feet and the image of another plane crash makes me shiver. I was ten. As someone shoved me out of the burning wreckage, I looked back, expecting it to be my mother stumbling out behind me. But it wasn't. I never saw my mother again. Even now, I can't help but wonder if she stood in that wreckage like this woman, searching for me, calling to me.

It's nightfall when the captain and his crew emerge from the woods. He surges toward me, his frame pearly white against the darkening forest.

"We found it! It's here!"

"Take me there."

He nods.

"Mark, I know where to find the box."

I'm surprised by the calmness of my voice. In moments, Mark Vincent, flanked by a handful of investigators, rushes toward me. I nod at the captain and he hurries into the woods. I follow, the others not far behind.

The captain leads me across the nettle-laden ground, deeper and deeper. His ghostly gleam is my only guidance. There, battered and hidden by brush, lies the small orange casing of the black box. I tear at the brush, pulling away branches and leaves until I have uncovered the box.

I step back as the investigators descend on it, gently lifting it from the foliage and carrying it back to the site. Mark hovers beside me. I walk behind the investigators as they carry the box out toward the trucks.

When I reach the site, I see the woman in denim still waiting. I close my eyes for a moment, feeling a closeness that makes my chest ache, and approach her. The woman holds the stuffed bear against her chest.

"Have you seen my daughter?" asks the woman. "I've been looking for her for hours!" Her ghostly face is tear-streaked and she looks utterly lost. "Please, where is my daughter?"

"She's in a hospital," I answer, my voice thin. "She survived the crash."

"Oh, thank God," the woman cries and slumps to the ground, clutching the bear. Her relief is overwhelming. "Thank God she's safe."

Shards of memories stab back into focus. A voice long-dead calls my name through the roar of fire, through shrill screams. But never have I been so far from that voice as I was that chilly October morning. Ten years have passed, but I clench my eyes closed, my mother's voice haunting my memory. How she shouted at me from the plane's burning wreckage, but they couldn't get to her in time. I inherited my curse that morning. Now, I relive every jet crash as if it were that awful October morning outside Spokane.

I drop to my knees, a sob tearing at my throat. I never saw my mother again. Never got to tell her goodbye. Why didn't she hear me? I called and called, but she never answered. If only she could have followed my voice to the exit. If only ice hadn't formed on the wings. My sobs wrench free, the rain pounding the ground now. If only.

While Mark and the others carry the black box toward a truck, Brittany walks out of the woods. Her form is translucent, milky and soft like fairy dust. I am afraid to move. I crouch there in the pouring rain.

"Mommy?"

The woman turns, her face contorting. "Oh, no! Oh, no, Brittany. I thought you were safe."

Her mother runs toward her and clasps the child to her chest. Sobbing, the little girl holds onto her mother. "I couldn't find you, Mommy. I couldn't find you!"

"Sssh, honey. It's all right." She lays the bear in Brittany's arms.

Shortly, Mark's cell phone rings. I watch the heaviness in his face. He shakes his head. A battle lost. He rushes into the debris and drops down beside me.

"The little girl passed away a few minutes ago," he shouts above the rain.

I nod and watch the last of the ghosts of flight 1155 melt into the woods and fade into the air. For a moment, Brittany's mother remains. She gazes at me as if she knows about my mother. There are no answers to these whys—to my whys—just acceptance, I realize.

"Could you—" I stop in mid-sentence.

She moves toward me and nods, urging me to continue.

"Could you tell my mother—that I miss her?"

"I'm sure she's already heard you."

The woman takes hold of her daughter's hand and slips after the others.

Peace settles warm and calm against my shoulders, as if someone has put an arm around me. My hands stop hurting. I pull off my gloves. The burns are receding . . . my gift is fading. I feel it. And for the first time, I understand this gift. I've been hearing my mother's voice for ten years—through these images. They were the goodbyes she never got to tell me.

I step out of the wreckage, knowing that tonight, I leave my gift behind. I trudge toward the investigators as they load the black box bound for D.C..

"They'll find that all engines failed," I tell them. "One engine caught fire and the other stopped working. The fire extinguishing system failed to come on-line, too. There was no evidence of pilot error. Goodnight."

I don't even turn to see their expressions. It doesn't matter if they believe me or not. They have the plane's flight record and I have mine. As I climb into my car, I look back at the forest and I wonder if a sparrow falls, does it rise again and sing?

THE SOUND OF ANGELS

Carrie leaned against the boat railing, Ellen's neuro-crosslink in her ear; Ellen wanted Carrie to be with her when she died today. Carrie gripped the edges of her teal windbreaker. Haro Strait in May was nippy, making her shiver.

The doctors had pinpointed Ellen's bodily functions to begin shutting down by 3 pm with the moment of death arriving at 4 pm. Ah, the wonders of modern medicine, Carrie thought. No scientific breakthroughs for curing cancer, but a new process to estimate the time of death.

Over the months, Ellen's condition had deteriorated, rendering her practically comatose. If it hadn't been for the neuro- crosslinks that Ellen had demanded be installed between them, Carrie wouldn't be able to be with Ellen now. She was a thousand miles away in a hospital bed while Carrie was out in the Puget Sound on a whale watching boat. Ellen had jokingly referred to the crosslink as a cellular phone.

'Buck up, love,' Ellen thought. 'You've been with me this long. Stay with me an hour more.'

A cold blackness hung inside Carrie, warmed only by the presence of Ellen's thoughts and feelings transmitted via satellite. Morphine-fogged images of their lakeside cottage fed into Carrie's already overloaded cortex.

'Why couldn't I stay with you, Ellen? In twelve years, this is the longest we've ever been apart? Why now?'

Ellen's tired voice whispered through her head as the cool breeze off the Strait pressed against her face. 'This will be the toughest hour of our relationship, kiddo. Stay with me, okay?'

Carrie fought down a sob and nodded. She watched the horizon, the blue blurring to green and back again. Cedars and firs framed the edge of the dark teal water. The hum of the boat resonated through her arms and into her chest. The air tasted of salt. It calmed her. There were less than a dozen people on this cruise, all of them keeping mostly to themselves. Off season was a good time to be here.

'Can you see the Sound, Ellen?'

Ellen had grown up here—on San Juan Island, near Friday Harbor—and hadn't been back in twelve years.

'When I was a kid—' Ellen paused and in a moment, pain rippled through Carrie, minimized for her by an endorphin filter. 'This water murmured peace and the dock boards echoed laughter,' Ellen continued. 'They still do—to anyone who'll listen. Are you listening?'

"I'm listening," Carrie whispered into the wind.

'I feel the motion of the boat. It's soothing. I'll miss boats.'

Carrie bit her lip, imagining Ellen's faraway smile, framed by honey-colored curls that were always too tight around her angular face. And her hazel eyes that conveyed so much more than her words. A tear streaked down Carrie's face and she quickly wiped it away. Her windbreaker rustled.

'No tears, kiddo. Not this trip.'

'Why won't you tell me why I'm out here? Tell me why I need to be here when I should be with you, Ellen?'

'I've already told you. To find the orcas. J-Pod.' Ellen paused. 'I feel the wind in my hair—' Another wave of pain. Carrie jerked, bumping the elbow of the woman next to her.

"I'm sorry."

"No harm done," the woman answered with a smile. She gripped a pair of binoculars and her floppy straw hat shadowed her face and glasses. "Is this your first time to see the whales?"

Carrie nodded. "Do you always see whales on these cruises?"

The woman shook her head and pushed the brim of her hat out of her eyes, revealing graying dark hair. "Not always, but I heard the Captain telling one of the crew that a pod of orcas was spotted near Stuart Island. That's where he's headed."

'Orcas, kiddo! Looks like my final wish has been granted.'

Tears trickled down Carrie's face again and she wiped them away. The woman squinted at her.

"Are you all right?"

"Fine."

The woman let the binoculars rest against her blue slicker. "It's okay. Lots of people get emotional on these trips. There's something special about orcas."

'Summer '78,' Ellen thought. 'Lime Kiln Point. My sister and I were sleeping on the warm rocks like a couple of lizards when I felt them in the water.'

'You're making that up,' Carrie thought.

She waited for Ellen's response. When none came, panic spiraled through her body, colder and tighter. She tapped frantically at the transmitter in her ear. 'Don't leave me! Ellen? Dear God, Ellen!'

Pain gouged her middle, even through the endorphin filter. Hunching over, she held onto the railing until it subsided.

"Maybe you'd better sit down," said the woman, a hand on Carrie's arm. "Until you're used to the boat."

Carrie nodded and allowed the woman to help her over to the bench.

"My name's Donna, Donna Ketcham."

"Carrie Brunner," she mumbled, her arms folded against her middle.

'I'm—here.'

'Ellen!' Carrie pinched her eyes closed. 'I'm sorry. I never realized how much pain you were in until now. Are you all right?'

'Fraid not, kiddo. It's 3:15. They say my kidneys are shutting down. I might not make 4 o'clock.'

Carrie rocked against the anguish mangling her heart.

'Be strong and listen. I want you to keep your eyes on the Sound.

21

No matter what. For the next forty-five minutes, you take in as much of the islands as you can. This is my last visit. Promise me.'

Carrie fought back the tears. 'I promise.'

'Good girl. I'll stay with you as long as I can. We had twelve good years, didn't we?'

'All of them!'

'Now, get back to that railing and watch for the whales.'

"I'm feeling better now," Carrie said to Donna. She rose from the bench and walked back to the railing.

Donna followed.

The water sparkled with sunlight as Carrie turned to the south to catch a glimpse of the Olympic Mountains. Mountain-framed islands with fir trees seemed unreal; the mist that hung over the islands at sunrise and sunset made them magical. On one of the smaller islands, a pair of Harbor seals sunned themselves on the rocks, their bulbous bodies oozing across the shoreline. The seals seemed unconcerned by the boat slipping past.

Slowly, Stuart Island drifted toward the boat. That's when she felt it. A soft, static electricity that brushed across her arms and down her spine. She moved to the front of the boat and leaned out. 'I feel something.' 'I know.' Carrie pictured Ellen's smirk and the wink in those mischievous hazel eyes. 'Listen to the water.'

A satiny black fin broke surface and a slick body arced through the dark teal water, a hint of white at its back. Carrie heard a soft, clear call, a mixture of melancholy and joy.

"They're so loud," said Carrie.

"Who's so loud?" Donna asked.

"The orcas," she answered. "See? Out there." She pointed, her windbreaker rasping.

Donna squinted. "I don't see anything. Much less hear anything."

Another fin, much larger than the first one, broke surface, joined immediately by two smaller fins. The droning sound deepened as the orcas rose and submerged again. They called a second time, haunting the water with pain and bliss.

Other people moved up to the front of the boat.

'Stay with me, Ellen.' Carrie stared at her watch. 3:38. 'Please stay with me.'

'Listen, kiddo. Listen.'

'Ellen, please . . . tell me why I'm here.'

'Soon enough, love. Listen.'

"Somebody said J-Pod was spotted very near here," Donna said and brought her binoculars up.

'The others won't see them yet.'

"There are three pods in this area: J, K and L. K-Pod is the smallest. J-Pod lost one of their adult males recently. The Captain said they've been acting funny ever since." Donna panned the horizon. "I can't see a thing."

Carrie stood motionless, riveted by the orca calls and the fins slicing through the water.

"Wait, I think I see something!" Donna bounced up and down in her deck shoes. "I see fins. Three of them! Right where you said, Carrie! Look!"

Carrie felt Ellen's life ticking away as the boat moved toward J-Pod.

'Look, kiddo. And listen.'

Slowly, the boat drew near to the orcas and when Carrie saw five or six of them, their sleek bodies humming through the water, the tears welled in her eyes. Joy washed over her, just like that snow-covered midnight when she had stepped into her first candlelit Mass on Christmas Eve and swore she could hear the angels singing in the rafters. The orcas' song echoed in her ears, and she felt it, understood it: mourning, acceptance, memory. They had accepted the death of a loved one and, honoring him, they went on, singing of him to anyone who listened.

Suddenly, their song widened, enfolding Carrie. They sang to her of Ellen, of her childhood, the pain they had carried since she had left them. And now their song soared with new joy: Ellen was back. Back through Carrie and the cross-link, if only for a little while. Carrie did not understand this closeness between the pod and Ellen, but she felt it, and was glad to be included, if only peripherally.

Two of the orcas rose up from the water, the white of their bellies showing as they seemed to almost stand straight up.

"Look, they're spyhopping!" Donna shouted.

Cameras clicked and people pointed. The orcas' faces held such fellowship that Carrie began to see the emotion reflected around her in the other passengers' faces. She watched the pod of passengers sharing binoculars and huddling together beside the railing. She felt herself drawing closer to these people and allowing them better views than she had for herself.

'Twelve years was a long time without them. I've missed them for so long.'

'Twelve years?'

'That's when I fell in love with you and left here. Listen.'

One of the orcas breached, black and white streaking out of the water. That set off a string of clicks and gasps. A lady moved out of the way so a toddler could see the whales. J-pod moved within six feet of the boat, veered around the bow and headed north toward Canada.

Carrie watched them disappear on the horizon, but she heard their whisper long after the fins had faded from view.

She felt the loss immediately, like her body was hollow. It was more than letting go of the whales. She looked down at her watch. 4:04 pm.

'Ellen?'

She waited. Water hummed against the boat. A pair of gulls called.

'Ellen?'

Wind whispered over the hull. A sandy-haired toddler giggled. Ellen was gone. Ellen with her special gift, the link with the orcas. A gift she'd had since childhood—that she'd given up without a word.

Carrie closed her eyes.

At last she understood why Ellen had sent her out here. It hadn't been for Ellen; it had been for her. Ellen had only wanted one last look at the place where she'd grown up and loved. The orcas had been for Carrie. The whisper of orcas and Ellen's voice undulated across the water.

Her tears welled. The trip hadn't been about letting go; it was about holding on. She had the courage to do that now. The orcas' song hung in her ears and for the first time in many, many months, she felt peace. She wasn't alone either. Ellen had made sure of that. She had passed on her link with the orcas and now, their communal presence lingered.

Slipping the transmitter out of her ear, she kissed the top.

"Goodbye, my love," she said and cast it into the Sound.

Scattering Ellen's memories instead of her ashes, Carrie thought. She could call them back by listening to the whispers on the waves, the laughter in the dock boards. She knew now why they called it the Sound.

MIDNIGHT OIL

Her spirit lamp burned in the grass beside the jack-o-lantern. Pumpkin orange flames dancing in the cold winter's night as she waited on the edge of the circle. They would come tonight as they did every eve of Beltane. Flames licking their smoky heels. Bass voices moaning above the clacking of dead leaves. Smoke charring the air. Dust rising. This time, their midnight gathering would end differently. The Witches of Beltane would come to reclaim those burned centuries before, luring out a victim to trade. Circles in the grass marked their point of combat. Their victim was her next door neighbor. They had filled his head with lies and now she waited, turning the spirit lamp down low. Finally, she knew their weakness.

At 11:45 pm, Jake Quillen awoke to screaming on his front lawn. Groggy, he crawled out of bed, throwing on his robe as he staggered down the stairs. A young teenager huddled on his stoop, stringy blond hair draped across powdery, tear-stained cheeks. Blood streaked her pink flannel nightshirt, drying like watercolors on her palms. She clutched his arm, grinding the terry-cloth against his skin until it burned.

"You've got to stop her," the teenager shouted.

Jake frowned. "Kerri, is this some sort of Halloween prank? Halloween isn't until tomorrow night and this kind of thing isn't funny."

"It's no prank, Jake," she shrieked. "She-she killed my dog."

His mouth gaped. "Who killed your dog?"

"Your neighbor, the witch, that's who! Look!" Kerri pointed at the dark green circle glistening on his front lawn. A tiny gray form slumped in its center.

"Reneta Ames killed your dog?"

Kerri nodded emphatically.

Several times this week, Jake had seen the woman burning an oil lamp on her patio, electric lights blazing behind her in the kitchen. Kerri and her friends had told everyone that the Ames woman stole neighborhood pets, prayed to the moon, and cast black magic in her backyard. Now, no one would go near her house. He didn't know what to believe.

"I'll call the police."

Kerri's grip tightened. "No, please," she urged, yanking him toward the yard. "Bury my dog first."

He gazed into the sad green eyes and nodded. First, a decent burial for Fifi and then a call to the police. Barefoot, he padded across the yard, Kerri a few paces behind him. When he reached the circle, Reneta Ames stepped out of the brush. Her sable hair was tied back from her face. She stood nearly as tall as Jake.

"Don't take another step," Reneta ordered, pointing at the circle's edge.

Jake halted in mid-stride. "What kind of monster are you?" he shouted. "Killing a kid's dog."

Her mahogany eyes widened and she turned her gaze to Kerri. "Tell him who killed the dog."

Kerri nudged Jake forward, hiding behind him. "Don't listen to her, Jake. My dog deserves a proper burial."

"Get her yourself, Kerri," said Reneta with a wry smile. "What's stopping you?"

"Jake," Kerri pleaded, her voice turning frail. "I'm frightened. Please make her leave. She's a witch, I tell you."

Ignoring Reneta, Jake stepped over the circle's edge and moved toward the dead animal. He bent toward the cold, stiff poodle's body and slid his fingers beneath it, but the body turned to ash in his hands. Something moved within the green circle. He turned. Shadowy figures rose from the earth. The air smelled of damp hay and dirt. Two thick, splintered poles punctured the earth, rising up into the cold night sky. Bundles of dry twigs lay around the bases of the wooden poles. Darkly-clothed figures streaked across the lawn and paused beside Kerri, skin whitewashed, eyes pinpoints of cruelty.

"The Beltane sisters," said Reneta with a sneer, "and right on time."

From the brush, she rolled out the flickering jack-o-lantern, sending Kerri and her sisters into hurried steps backward. The gray figures mixed with the darkness like ashes on slate. Voices, deep and desperate reverberated around Jake in raspy whispers.

Jake tried to escape the circle, but the twigs coiled around his legs, forcing him against the stake.

"It seems we're having a bonfire in your honor, Jake," Kerri said with a steely laugh.

Hands like wisps of darkness held Jake against the stake.

"Kerri . . . why?"

"Every eve of Beltane, the earth yields up the ashes of my sisters burned at the stake. Only a trade of human spirit will free them from their circles."

"She's been collecting them all over the country," said Reneta, backing away.

Kerri reached into the sky and plucked a spark from it. She rolled it around in her palm and then threw the spark at the twigs. Jake screamed as oily black smoke rose up in a wide shaft followed by a ring of crimson flames. Heat roiled against Jake's face, chafing cheeks, scorching robe.

Spirits moaned until a shrill, piercing scream rippled through the stillness. The terrified spirit of a bound woman plunged up from the earth and hovered beside Jake, her hair and body set aflame. He smashed his eyes closed as the burning spirit wailed in agony.

Reneta slipped back to the brush and slid out the spirit lamp, the oil base nearly empty. Another grating scream ripped through the silence, startling Jake. He opened his eyes and kicked at the flames. Skin blistered. The spirits wept. Others leaped up from the dirt, flames wild and pitching. Reneta turned the wick up until the spirit lamp's umber flames danced in the night air.

"What are you doing?" Kerri shrieked and stepped back. "Take it away, do you hear! Take it away!"

Reneta waved the lamp at the Beltane Witches. Kerri drew her arm over her face, stumbling back from the circle.

"Don't fear it, ladies. Look closer."

When Reneta was an arm's distance from Kerri, she swept off the globe. Instantly, Kerri was mesmerized by the flame. With wide, crimson eyes, she watched it flicker and sway in the darkness. Her solid form began to fade. Skin turned translucent. Finally, her body dissipated into a wisp of smoke drawn into the lamp's flame. The clear oil turned red, the level rising a half inch. One by one, the other witches turned to smoke, followed by the burning spirits. Ribbons of smoke slithered into the lamp until the oil's base brimmed with crimson oil. The fire at Jake's feet quickly fizzled and sank into the earth. With a groan, the stake receded back into the earth, leaving Jake standing alone in the center of the yard. Somewhere in the distance, a dog barked. He could only stare at her, dumbfounded.

Reneta held out the lamp to him. "It's a Spirit lamp. Dark Witches like the Beltane sisters fear fire but are drawn to it like moths. Fire forges good from evil. What isn't good burns away. That's why a white witch cannot burn." She held a finger in the flame, making Jake wince, but her skin did not even redden.

"Kerri sure played me for a fool," Jake said with a sigh. "I thought you were victimizing her."

Reneta shook her head. "She knew you would never suspect a child—especially with me there to blame." She motioned him across the yard toward her house. "Care to burn a little midnight oil?"

Jake smiled. "Love to."

They talked about All Hallow's Eve and the Salem witch trials. Reneta told him all about the Witches of Beltane, their annual gatherings and their fear of fire. When morning came, the oil lamp was empty. Reneta gave Jake the jack-o-lantern with its thick white candle inside to ward off the Witches of Beltane. There were many more than those who appeared on his lawn. Gratefully, Jake accepted it.

Every Halloween, a smiling jack-o-lantern burns on Jake's porch to keep the Witches of Beltane away from his door.

WILD FEED

Javelin missiles hissed through black smoke. Mortars exploded above the gnawing growl of machine gun fire raking the dusty streets below. Thick smoke coiled like a python around the Black Hawk helicopter descending toward a city that Davy Cullan couldn't even pronounce.

Davy gripped his —4 carbine and waited for landing. His very first.

His flak jacket was heavy and hot. Surrounding him in nervous silence were ten guys from his combat team. Davy touched the cross at his neck, his lips moving in soundless prayer, and tried to forget the camera attached to his helmet. The Hollywood sound stage he'd spent weeks on before shipping out seemed a lifetime away now. As surreal as this drop into hell.

"Approaching drop point. Get ready to move out on my order!" Davy's CO called through the copter.

He'd been interviewed by the hosts of the U.S.'s favorite TV show and tapes of his life and basic training were shown to the audience. America voted him into the finals. He was one of the favorites, they told him. Now, the footage he was transmitting back to the West would air live on national television. Wild feed, the Hollywood types called it. They had no fucking clue.

Hard-edged guitar riffs and wild drumbeats blared through the TV, the grunged metallic logo of REAL-TV's On-The-Job Hero hitting

31

the screen. Digital, high definition, real-time information with real people in real danger. Warning: Contains violence. Scenes may be too graphic for some viewers.

Clutching the armrest, Mary Cullan sat frozen on the blue couch beside her husband Ryan, her stomach an over-wrapped rubber band. Her fourteen-year-old daughter Tracy sat on the floor hugging her knees (there had been no stopping her from viewing tonight's show). Ryan held his bottle of Bud Light in a white-knuckled death grip as Hollywood hosts, India Haworth and Vic Baylor took the stage to massive applause.

"Hello, America!" India shouts and shakes her pale blonde hair. Her sequined blue dress stops at mid-thigh on her tall, waifish frame. "Welcome to On-The-Job Hero!"

Mary hated her unaffected, glittering smile.

Twenty-something Vic Baylor in his gray suit coat and t-shirt takes a step toward the audience. He reminded her of a mannequin in hip jeans.

"Each week, On-The-Job Hero follows three people chosen by you, America!" The audience cheers. "Police officers, firefighters, soldiers. People who risk their lives everyday at work compete to earn $200,000 by becoming an On-The-Job Hero."

The camera pans to India. She shakes her long hair. *How much of those tresses were wigs and extensions*, Mary wondered. "And remember, every week, you—" She points toward the camera, smiling. "That's right, you, America get to judge their perfor-mances. Only *you* can pick the *next*. On-The-Job. Hero. And at Real-TV, it's real life, real time, all-the-time."

"Why do they talk so much?" Tracy asked, looking toward her mother. "I want to see Davy."

Ryan took a sip of his beer. "To torture us," he mumbled with a scowl.

Vic Baylor's perfect chic let teeth flash in an over-bright grin, "That's right, India Only on Real-TV," says Vic, his tone melo-dramatic, "do you—America—get *real* information. *As* it happens."

Pictures of three contestants flash across the screen behind the hosts as they move to two plush, comfortable chairs at the edge of the stage.

Mary held her breath when the clip of a brown-haired young man in Army fatigues, saluting, ran behind the hosts. Her son's image cut through her; she gripped Ryan's hand. "Oh, God."

"There's Davy!" Tracy shouted, pointing at the TV.

Ryan sighed, his eyes closing for a moment.

India sits, crossing her legs carefully to avoid a wardrobe malfunction. Vic sits in the other chair and leans back in his most dramatic, Emmy-nominated pose.

"To recap," says Vic, "last week saw Mississippi police officer Christine Davis wreck her squad car in a high speed car chase."

Twisted metal, flashing lights, and rain-slicked streets appear behind Vic.

"Christine received the least votes, so she isn't among tonight's three finalists. She remains in stable condition in a Baton Rouge hospital and we wish her well. Right, everyone?"

Wild applause from the audience.

Mary shook her head in disbelief, hoping Officer Davis would be okay. *What was Davis thinking to wreck like that*, Mary thought, shocked by the callousness. *That coma wasn't in the script. Besides, it was bad for ratings. No wonder they voted her off.*

The camera shifts to India and she leans toward the camera with her best glossy pout. "Three contestants remain: New York City police officer Tony Vance."

A still picture of a thirtyish, dark-haired man with a jaded smile fades onto the screen behind India.

"Pose for us, India," said Mary, rolling her eyes. "So we forget that horrible accident."

"Shelly Renaldo, a San Francisco firefighter." Renaldo's solemn, twenty-something expression touches the screen, her auburn hair cut short around her face.

Vic takes over the list. "And nineteen-year-old Private Davy Cullan, from Indiana, who's stationed in the Middle East."

Wide-eyed, proud, and eager, Davy's boyish face appears, flaxen hair covered by a helmet. Mary's heart pounded into her throat as she grabbed a pillow and cradled it in her lap, remembering the patrols, the car bombs, and the endless fighting. Davy was a new recruit, barely out of high school and boot camp. He'd never fought in a war before.

But she and Ryan had. She glanced at her husband's glazed expression, taut mouth, and unrelenting grip on his Bud Light, the battles still playing behind his eyes. She understood those afterimages. The Iraq War. And two decades later, it was still going on. Now, it was her son's generation's turn to fight it. Her chest ached at the thought, but she'd been there. She knew what her son was going through. How trivial Vic and India made it all appear. She hated this show, but if it brought her images of Davy, she'd suffer through it.

"And remember," says India in a perky voice, that plastic smile unwavering. "There are many ways to vote for your favorite hero: online at www dot onthejobhero—that's one word, no spaces—dot com. You can also vote by phone and by pager."

Cameras pan the audience who hold up Sharpie-drawn, glitter-filled signs for contestants. Mary couldn't help but smile at two that read, "Davy Rocks!" and "Davy's My Hero!"

Vic waves his arm toward the screen. "We now take you live, via Real-TV's patented wild feed, to see our three contestants in action. First up is Private Davy Cullan." His voice takes on a hushed, faux dramatic tone as if he were at a golf tournament. "He's about to see combat for the very first time. We take you live to a battlefield in the Middle East. Through Davy Cullan's eyes."

Right on cue, Vic's face turns out a solemn, fashion model stare. "A day in the life of a combat soldier."

Automatic weapon fire intensified, almost drowning out the beat of helicopter blades until the Black Hawk's dark descent halted with a thump against pavement.

Streets. Davy swallowed hard. He'd be fighting the enemy in city streets.

He was proud to serve his country, but fear hung deep inside. What would it be like to stare down his sights at another soldier?

He'd never been in combat before, not like his parents. But they both made it home. He just hoped he did things right.

Doors swung open. Smoke roiled into the hold, explosions rocking the copter. For several moments he couldn't see First Lieutenant Cooper.

"Move out! Go, go, go!"

Davy lurched forward, his grip iron against his —4 as he scrambled through the opening and onto pavement.

Bullets zinged past, machine gun fire strafing the broken pavement. Davy concentrated on his CO's voice and the man in front of him as he ran, disoriented through smoke, —4 raised and head down. Machine gun rounds chewed up concrete and tore up buildings, including the one he was running toward.

Ahead, a yawning doorway appeared and disappeared in the roiling smoke. Behind him, boots pounded the pavement. The rest of his combat team, dropped in like he'd been dropped.

In an instant, he was inside a building. Bullets whizzed past the doorway, gouging the stone walls. Davy pressed his back to the wall, —4 raised as he scanned for enemy forces.

Someone screamed. He jerked his head toward the opening, —4 raised, chest pounding with dread, sweat coating his face.

"Lieutenant, Stevens is hit!" Two of the soldiers pulled Stevens inside the building. His right leg and side were blood-soaked and bullet-torn.

Harris, a platoon sergeant, laid Stevens against the wall and elevated his right leg. His dark skin was sweat-slicked and splotched with Stevens' blood.

"Hang on, Stevens," he said in a deep, calming voice, laying a hand against Stevens' shoulder, carbine wedged against his right shoulder as he scanned for the enemy. "We'll get you out of here."

"Cullan!" Harris shouted. "Field dressing for Stevens."

Davy dropped down on one knee beside Stevens and pulled a field dressing from Stevens' dropped rifle stock. (They taped dressings on the stock for quick access.) His hands shook, but they remembered what his months of training had taught him. Davy placed the dressing over Stevens' wounded right leg, tied the edges of the dressing, then slid two fingers under the knot to check the tightness. Stevens winced, gritting his teeth, but he didn't cry out.

Sergeant Harris' dark eyes were a mixture of sadness and determination. "I'll radio in our position and try for an evac." He disappeared up the line toward Lieutenant Cooper.

Davy nodded, glancing at Stevens' leg and the blood-soaked bandage. He was bleeding hard.

"Call in an air strike and medevac!" Sergeant Harris shouted. "We're pinned down in here and I've got a man down!"

The camera fades to a close-up of India Haworth looking grim but perky. Until the next botox shot, Mary thought frowning at the cutaway from Davy.

"Private Davy Cullan is facing a life or death situation and is bravely trying to save the life of his fellow soldier." The camera angle changes and she turns her head, still looking grim but perky into camera two.

Mary hoped the two cameras didn't confuse the poor thing.

"Now, let's check in on Firefighter Shelly Renaldo and see how her day is shaping up. Vic?"

Vic smoothes his hair and flashes his chiclet grin. A three-alarm fire, such happy occasion. Mary bet all firefighters grinned like that when they went to fires.

"While we took you to the Middle East, Shelly Renaldo was en route to a three-alarm fire near Fisherman's Wharf. Let's join her now."

Mary rose from the couch, unable to sit still. Anything could be happening to Davy while they cut to the San Francisco feed! She hated this show, but couldn't stop herself from watching. Her son was out there and good or bad, she couldn't stand hearing the news from a neighbor. Although, hearing it from India Haworth's mouth wasn't much better.

"Dad, will Davy be okay?" Tracy asked, fear shining in her eyes.

Ryan's bottom lip quivered and he set his beer bottle on the coffee table. "He's got a good chance, Trace. A real good chance." He ran a shaking hand through his thinning blond hair.

Mary barely watched Shelly Renaldo breaking down a door with an axe and entering a burning building. Slender and fearless, she moved ahead, shouting for anyone inside.

Mary thought of the woman's mother and father seeing this live in Bakersfield or Portland—like her and Ryan. Or later that evening on the 11 o'clock news. The public had a right to know, or so the journalists always spouted. She didn't know if anyone had the right to know this much about other people's lives, but this was too much. Too much information.

Just as Shelly reaches a mother and daughter on a smoke-filled third floor, Vic, looking concerned, announces a cut to commercial. Another Emmy-winning close-up. Mary wanted to wretch.

Soup commercials, paper towels, and drugs she'd never heard of but was told to ask her doctor about scrolled endlessly across the screen. Mary crossed her arms and paced, desperate to know if her son was all right. Was he safe? Did he save that other soldier's life? She didn't care about cat litter and new cars. She wanted to know that Davy was still alive.

Guitar riffs and drumbeats announce India's presence at center stage, her blonde hair freshly spritzed and scrunched.

"Welcome back," she says, her lipstick still sparkling. India walks dramatically across the stage. "A police officer never knows when danger is hiding behind the next door. We now join Officer Tony Vance as he and his partner respond to a domestic violence call."

Almost instantly, Officer Vance and his partner fall into a stand-off with a crazed man holding his wife at knife point.

"Put down the knife!" Vance shouts at the dark doorway, thin trickle of street lights illuminating a man's pudgy frame.

"I can't watch," Tracy said with a groan, covering her eyes. In a few moments, she rose from the floor and plopped down beside her dad, hiding her face. "Tell me when Davy's back on."

"This is ridiculous," Mary said as a woman screamed and a shot was fired.

Mary snatched the remote from Ryan and changed the channel. Lions of Africa. A group of lionesses stalked a baby antelope. Click. A movie station, showing *Seven* for the seventh time this week. Click.

"Ten soldiers were killed today when—"

Click.

"Severe weather alerts continue today for much of—"

Mute. Silence.

Exhausted, Mary sank down beside Ryan on the couch as the TV images rushed by in silence. The refrigerator compressor clattered then fell silent. The air conditioner fan shut off. The house creaked. For several minutes, Mary listened to her own breath rising and falling. The bombardment hurt her brain and she shut it all out, letting the silence stretch longer and longer until she could almost deal with a tiny piece of it.

"Mom," said Tracy, a hand on her arm.

She turned to her daughter, but didn't speak.

"Mom, do you think they've switched back to Davy yet?"

She studied Tracy's intense brown gaze, so much like Davy's. What was he seeing right now? Mary didn't want to turn it back on, but not knowing about Davy was too much. She reached for the remote and flicked it on again, flipping back to On-The-Job Hero. She was almost relieved to see the Gorton fisherman.

"Now, America, it's your turn to vote. Vote now for your favorite hero," says Vic.

"Who will it be?" India asks and gestures toward all three contestants' pictures on the screen. "Police Officer Vance and the stand-off? Firefighter Renaldo and a burning building? Or Private Cullan and the injured soldier?"

"After the commercial break," Vic continues, running a hand through his hair. "We will show the wild feed for your choice, America."

Tracy leaped up from the couch and ran toward the computer on the kitchen desk. Ryan slid his pager out of his pocket while Mary grabbed the phone, all of them casting votes for Davy. Mary stabbed the numbers, frustrated by the busy signals until she finally got through. Hanging up, she started over again. Over and over until India Haworth's voice echoed from the TV.

"Okay everyone," she says and gestures toward the screen behind her where all three contestants' pictures are still displayed. "We've tallied your votes. This week's choice is—"

She pauses and the audience is on their feet, clapping and shouting names.

"This week's choice is: Private Davy Cullan! Let's get back to Private Cullan and the injured soldier!"

Mary, Ryan, and Tracy dropped down in front of the TV, waiting for the feed to transmit Davy's situation.

"Repeat, we're pinned down. Requesting air strike at these coordinates . . . "

Davy turned his attention back to Stevens. He'd used a second pressure bandage and Stevens' wound kept bleeding. Davy opened the shoulder pouch on Stevens' vest and retrieved a biohemostat bandage. That was the guy's best chance of not losing his leg. The wound-sealing, advanced pressure bandage should exert enough pressure to stop the bleeding. He applied it quickly.

Mortar fire shook the building. The far wall cracked and hunks of plaster and stone rained down on them. Machine gun fire pummeled an interior wall and bullets exploded around them.

Something slammed into Davy's chest and hip, propelling him backward. His helmet cracked against the wall and he was sinking. His chest burned. He hit the ground, falling beside Stevens' still form. The high tech bandage stopped the bleeding, but not the spray of bullets. Stevens was gone.

"Stevens," he called, shaking the young man's arm. "Dammit, Stevens is dead!"

"Davy—oh God—Davy!" Mary saw her son's bloody hand through the helmet camera pulling at the dead soldier. She prayed that Stevens' mother wasn't watching like she was right now.

Davy's camera lolled back and forth, showing only the scuffle of boots and ricochet of bullets against plaster walls.

"Davy, boy, get up," Ryan shouted through gritted teeth. "You're not finished yet."

Wide-eyed, Tracy clung to her dad's arm, tears slipping down her cheeks.

The tangle of enemy voices mixed with gun fire and the shouts of his platoon. A distant hope underneath the chaos was the steady voice of Sergeant Harris calling in an air strike, reinforcements, medevac—anything.

Davy pulled himself to a sitting position against the wall and scooped up his —4. From the broken doorway, an enemy soldier rushed toward him, raising an AK-47 to his shoulder.

Squeezing off several rounds, Davy dropped the soldier to his knees only four feet in front of him. The soldier triggered a few rounds, but his gun was aimed at the floor now. Bullets tore into the concrete as the soldier collapsed, his beige speckled uniform turning dark with blood.

"Hold your positions!" Lieutenant Cooper shouted through the building.

"Help's on the way," Sergeant Harris' voice rang out.

The —4 was too heavy and Davy let it fall against his legs as he sank onto the floor again. He listened for the familiar beat of Black Hawks descending from the sky to carry him out of this hell. Then he remembered the camera on his helmet.

"Mom . . . Dad, Tracy . . . if you're hearing and seeing this—I'm gonna be okay."

Harris was beside him now, cutting through vest and straps to get to his chest wounds.

"But—just in case something happens, all my love. And I'll see you soon."

Mary couldn't halt her tears. She reached out toward the screen as if she could touch Davy's face. Ryan's hand was against her arm. With his other arm, he cradled Tracy against his shoulder. She knew his pain was tight in his palm. If he let her go, he would let it all go raging forward.

A soldier hangs over Davy, working feverishly with bandages.

"Don't you go anywhere on me, Cullan." He smiles. "Otherwise, they'll be takin' this expensive bandage out of my paycheck."

"I'm staying right here, Sarge," says Davy.

Suddenly, the soldier glances toward the ceiling, the smile still on his face. He leans down toward Davy.

"You hear that?"

"What?" Davy asks, his voice ragged.

"It's the blessed sound of Black Hawks."

"Then we're gettin' outta here," says Davy. "Awright."

Bullets whiz through the building and the soldier ducks, covering Davy. When no more bullets hit, the soldier sits up, reaching for him.

"Let's get out of here, Private."

"They're getting out!" Mary cried, wiping tears from her face.

"I knew somebody'd come in for 'em," said Ryan. "No one gets left behind."

Something clattered across the floor and rolled to a stop about six feet from Davy. His whole body went cold.

A grenade. With no pin.

"Grenade, Sarge!"

A blinding flash then dead air.

The white noise was salt in the wound as Mary stared at the dark TV screen, seconds expanding then at last, standing still until Ryan's sobs rose above Tracy's aching cries.

Mary couldn't process it yet. *It was just television, right? No one's really dead on TV.* The numbness spread through her in pain-stopping waves.

An ad for antiperspirant raced across the screen, bleeding into fruit juice and lunch meat and the latest fitness craze. It all moved around her so fast then surged on, like nothing had happened. Like her son hadn't just died in front of millions of viewers.

Finally, India's somber but smiling face fills the screen, her pout freshly glossed, her eyes glassy with eye drops. *But the show must go on. The public has a right to know.*

With an anguished scream, Mary slammed her fist against the TV's off button and threw the remote against the screen. The noise and lights and pain faded into numbness. Sometimes that was just too much.

HOMECOMING

I buried my baby today. Perfect with her ten, delicate fingers and ten, tiny toes. Beautiful with her downy, black hair covering her round, little head. If only I could have seen life in her blue eyes or heard a shriek burst from her lungs. Here in the colony, there is only one doctor for every settlement. They have the technology to bring people to Mars, but not enough to save one baby born prematurely.

The sun set an hour ago, shrouding our small biosphere in an uneasy silence that thickens with the darkness. I insisted that Mansi be buried in our biosphere. Already, the wild flowers on her grave are wilting. Beyond the biosphere, the night is calm, chilly. The scent of dust and dry heat presses up from the ground as the sand whispers beneath my feet. It is the only sound I can make.

Kneeling at the grave, I pluck out pottery-like shards from the mound of red dirt covering my baby, Mansi. The smooth, deep ochre shards, some as large as my palm, are everywhere on Mars. I scatter them away from the grave. They clatter against each other, hollow and restless, like Mansi's spirit.

Questions tear at me as I wrap my arms around my body, my abdomen still swollen and thick. Why . . . why *my* baby, my first child? Instead of feeling the link that once joined Mansi to me, there is only emptiness and aching. I want to scream at the stars that have risen in the Martian sky and chase them away. My daughter has joined Those Gone Before and I hate that most of all. They are forgotten and now, she will be, too. Just a name in a registry and a sad headstone showing not even one day of life.

"Chasovi!"

Hanu's voice startles me. His hurried footsteps echo through the biosphere, fading into the waves of red dust undulating across the dark, cold desert. I hate the cold beyond our biosphere. It feels so close tonight.

He calls for me again, his voice raspy and desperate. He races across the desert toward me.

"Chasovi, please," he says, out of breath. His strong hands grip my arms as he slides down beside me. "Dr. Jeffries says you need to stay in bed. Please, come back inside."

"Soon," I say, "when I know her spirit is settled."

He slips his arm around my shoulders, but I retreat from his touch. His tanned, thin face is haggard and his watery dark eyes are deeply circled. His usually neatly combed walnut hair, tied at his shoulders swings free. This loss has aged him. He has always been strong and graceful like the sandstone mesas of the Acoma pueblo we left behind, but tonight, I see such pain in his eyes. It is something I've never before seen in him.

He studies the grave for a moment. Finally, tears slip down his cheeks and through quivering lips, he sings an Acoma prayer of peace to our daughter. He reaches for me again and this time, I go to him, putting my voice to his.

Sharp pain slices through my abdomen and I cry out, everything blurring. Hanu's voice fades from my ears then erupts in shouting. Someone leans over me and I force my eyes open.

"Chasovi, do you hear me?" Hanu cries, wiping away tears. "Chasovi, please!"

I nod.

"Let me take you home." He lifts me from the sand with the gentleness of the wind.

Every step causes me pain, but I continue to sing the old Acoma prayer for Mansi, my voice hoarse and broken. Soon, cactus shadows fall across the wooden deck of our house as Hanu hurries across it. Hanu doesn't like the desert, but cactuses grow well here and they remind him of our mesa village on Earth. The Sky City, as we've always called it, for beyond the mesa there is only sky, deep blue and endless. But this dry, dead world with its vast amber sky is my home, now that Mansi—part of me—lies here. The deck boards creak with Hanu's steps as he opens the door.

The hallway is dark, the murmur of the vid-unit growing louder as Hanu enters the bedroom and lays me on the bed. I reach up to him, but his worried face fades into darkness as I close my eyes in exhaustion and sleep.

A baby's rattle, made from a gourd and carried on the back of a badger, clacks through my dreams. Behind the badger stand two animals in shadow. The mesa beneath their feet begins to crumble, the dry clack of seed against gourd deepening, until the gourd shatters, littering the red sands with finger-sized fragments.

My eyes open and I sit up, the covers jumbled around me. Mansi's spirit is unsettled. Badger, keeper of stories, has carried her restlessness to me. My body hurts as I reach for Hanu, but he isn't there.

"Hanu?"

He steps out of the bathroom, his long, walnut hair tied back. His lithe form is graceful in his linen pants and shirt as he slips into a white, environmental suit.

"How do you feel, Chasovi?" he asks, offering a smile that fades as quickly as it appears.

How do I feel? Empty. Broken. "Will you help me out to the grave?"

His brow furrows. "What?"

"I dreamed of her restless spirit, Hanu," I tell him and shakily rise to my feet. "Badger brought me her story. We must say the old prayers until her spirit has quieted or she will never have peace."

Hanu sighs. "Chasovi, don't. You've done all you can for Mansi. The old ways help no one anymore." Always, he turns away from the old ways.

"Why did she come to us too soon, Hanu? Why?"

He takes me in his arms and holds me so tight that I feel like I'm holding him up. "I don't know, 'Sovi. I don't know. I don't know why we ever came here."

I pull away. "To carry our Acoma ancestors forward. To bring their stories here. To bring hope home to the pueblo. Why do you question that now?"

"Always you speak of the old stories." His eyes darken. "Of the tribe. Of our ancestors! What about us, 'Sovi? You and me! What of the home we left behind—for this backward place?"

"I thought _this_ was our home."

"And I thought we were moving forward, not backward in time." He runs thick fingers through his bangs and holds out his arms. "I wanted to upload her picture and send it back to the pueblo. I wanted to hold her in my arms and tell her of the mesas and blue sky where I grew up. I wanted to sing new songs to her." He sighs. "Not an old prayer of peace."

I cannot comfort him. I feel drained.

He grits his teeth. "We'll never have another child!"

I shake my head, but I can only think of Mansi. "In time—"

He takes my hands in his. "No, 'Sovi. Doctor Jeffries said this birth damaged your womb. He said you may never be able to carry another child."

I pull away, his words cutting through me. "What are you saying?"

"I didn't want him to tell you," Hanu says, unable to look me in the eye. "I thought it would be less painful coming from me."

I grab hold of the bed to steady myself, unwilling to believe him.

Hanu cups my face in his hands. "'Sovi, maybe we could have another baby if we returned to Earth?" His expression brightens and the shadows retreat from his face. "They have facilities for—"

"No," I snap. "My home—our home is here. It was our tribe's wish to be among the first colonists. It's our duty to stay." I squint against the sting of tears. "Besides, Mansi is here." And her unsettled spirit that must be quieted.

His face pinches with frustration. "I've already requested our resignation from the colony. It's decided. There's a transport leaving in less than a week, Chasovi. We're going to be on it."

"You'll do so without me then!" I shove past him into the bathroom and slam the door, locking it.

"We'll talk about it tonight," he announces, ignoring my words. "I'm going to work now." In a moment, there is only silence beyond the door.

Outside the biospheres, there are many caves with strange symbols embedded in the walls and stone formations. They were left by Those Gone Before. Unlike my people, an entire race rose up here, prospered, and died on these red sands. Except for the glyphs and pottery shards, there is no other record of them here. Every week, as part of our colony duties, Hanu and I and a few others journey out to the caves to study the glyphs and shards. None of the scholars can agree on the glyphs' meanings. That's why Hanu and I were chosen to be among the colonists. Our ancestors left behind similar depictions on cave walls, symbols from a dying language that few remember. It is the scholars' hope that, because of our heritage, Hanu and I will understand these symbols.

Translation work will keep my mind occupied, so I dress in beige linen pants and tunic and slide into my own environmental suit. I move through the narrow hallway toward the airlock and put on my gloves and helmet. Still feeling weak, I hurry out into Mars's cold expanse.

Morning washes maroon and amber across the rocky landscape with its stone formations. I hate being in this suit. Would this place smell gritty and dry, like the sandstone mesas—a hint of sweet grass and sage dusting the air?

Reminds me of the walks I took back at the mesa with Mother to dig out clay. Her pottery was so vivid—smooth baked clay with crisp black cloud swirls and raindrops on a terra-cotta background. She spent hours grinding her new clay, never letting me forget that clay was stone that had to be tempered just right with the old ways. So, with rounded stones, she took shards of her ancestors' pottery, some hundreds of years old, ground them to a fine powder, and mixed it with the clay. Like Hanu and I being part of this colony. Tempering their technology with the old ways, deciphering dead glyphs with a dying language. It allows both to survive, so I welcome it.

A pathway twists through a field of boulders and toward the clusters of caves nearest our biosphere. Hanu prefers the line of caves an hour's walk from here. The landscape is stark and ruddy, but there is silent strength to this world. It reminds me of the Acoma sandstones. Hanu wanted to go far from our pueblo, wanting to move our small village into the future, casting off the old ways, but this place, he says, has set us back hundreds of years. From the glyphs I have studied, I fear the Acoma pueblo is treading the same path as Those Gone Before—perhaps even this colony.

There are so many stories about why the Martian world is barren—cataclysms, meteorites—famine. The glyphs point to something else, though, something I only feel inside but can't articulate.

Even out here, I feel Mansi's restless spirit. My steps quicken, but her restlessness stays with me. I have to help her and soon. She has suffered enough in her short life.

The ruddy sky grows hazy and the temperature cools as the stone formations cast thick shadows across the cave entrance. The ridge is ringed with bands of maroon and amber, reminding me of wood grain. I flick on my helmet lamp and enter the cave.

It is a shallow chamber shaped like a spoon. On the back wall, delicate symbols gleam almost silver in the dim light. They emboss the rocky surface with a series of swirls and slashes. I imagine a terse language with guttural syllables sharply spoken. Hurried strokes, arranged in columns that seem to take on odd shapes—almost triangle-like in their arrangement.

I move to the last grouping and lay my gloved hand against the longest string of symbols. The scholars and the other colonists try to read these left to right or right to left, but for this place, that feels wrong somehow. So I try to read them up and down—column by column.

In the gleaming slashes and swirls, I see glyphs from mother's pottery: stepped clouds, rain, plants. Then I see rabbit among the glyphs. In the next column, bits of Keresan words touch me. I see Acoma in these glyphs and I miss making pottery with my mother and grandmother. Tears trickle down my face. Mansi will never know these things and I will never get to teach her as mother taught me. The emptiness in my belly aches and I feel her restless spirit again. Angry, I clutch at the symbols.

Why my baby—why, Great Spirit? Why do you send the keeper of stories to me when Mansi's ended before it began? My questions go unanswered. I drop to my knees and sob, pounding the dust.

Abruptly, a low thrum rises and falls through the chamber. Light dims to near darkness and back again. I reach out to the glyphs. They have changed color—a soft gold sheen covers them now.

The thrumming sound radiates through the chamber and my suit until I feel the notes resonating in my chest. I get to my feet and press both gloved hands to the walls. In my Keresan tongue, I singsong the words to an Acoma story ritual the storytellers recite to children. I murmur of badger and the Great Star Nation, of stars being stories and of new lights in the evening sky.

Some of the glyphs take on meaning that I feel more than I see. Part of their story—Those Gone Before—fills my senses. Sweet grasses and rivers, mud flats and villages formed of red clay and ruddy loam. Of advances and great cities. A time of leaving.

My eyes widen and I let the story ritual's words fade to silence. This world wasn't uninhabitable. It was abandoned for greater worlds and newer ways. The old ways died, not the people.

As I stare at a fan-shaped shard that lies in the dust at my feet, the story continues. The protectors of the old ways, in some ritual of binding, sealed their life forces into the stone formations of their ancestors, hoping that some day, their people would return to the old ways and need the guidance of Those Gone Before. But they never returned. Formations grew brittle, crumbling, as the world died. The ritual of return lies dormant along with the shards of Those Gone Before.

My mind races at these stories and the ritual of return. I press my hands harder against the glyphs, hoping to learn more of this ritual of return, but the thrumming sounds have hushed now and the glyphs' silvery gleam has returned. They've told me all they will tell me now.

I lean down and pluck the fan-shaped shard from the dust. I

remember rabbit among the glyphs, showing me new life. Then the words of my mother echo in my head. "Life is always a gift, even if it only lasts a moment, because that moment brings a new star into the heavens. Life force sleeps, life force disperses, but it never dies."

Mansi's restlessness trembles through me and looking at this shard, I, at last, understand. My eyes well with tears. All this time, she's been trying to tell me, but I haven't been listening. It isn't just *her* spirit that is restless. The life forces within these shards are restless. It is this entire world that must be quieted.

I throw down the shard and run out of the cave. I know what I must do.

Returning to the biosphere, I find it empty. Hanu has not returned from the easternmost caves yet. It is just as well. He does not believe in the ancient Acoma rituals any more, just the new rituals of interstellar travel and computers.

I hurry into the bedroom and retrieve my satchel from the closet. Inside are the ceremonial things I had prepared to welcome Mansi into our lives. I rush to the airlock and remove my environmental suit. After thrusting the suit back into its compartment, I hurry outside, onto the deck.

Among a half moon of cactuses and sweet grass stands Mansi's grave. I kneel and then lay my hand against the mound. Already, my tears fall. She was so beautiful. How I yearn to know who she would have been. I miss Mansi. I miss the things she will never do and the woman she will never become.

As my mother quiets the restless spirits of our ancestors by making them part of a new vessel, so will I do for my daughter and Those Gone Before. Grinding the clay, tempering it with shards of an ancient vessel, its clay long crumbled but well-mixed, and then molding that clay into a new vessel. It is the only thing I can do for them now.

From my satchel, I take a bundle of dried sage and matches. I light the bundle and lay it on Mansi's grave. The sweet, husky scent swirls around me.

I take a long, flat grinding stone from the satchel and lay the stone in front of me. From the dusty ground, I draw out a handful of shards and lay them on the stone. That will be enough.

Also, from the satchel, I take a scrap of soft pink linen. Wrapped within its folds is a piece of dried umbilical cord that had once joined Mansi and me. Tears drip down my face, but I wipe them back and go on, laying the bit of cord on top of the shards.

Then I pick up a smooth, round stone as big as my fist and crumble the cord and ancient shards.

I pause to pick up the bundle of burning sage. Its heady scent fills me with courage. I raise the bundle of sage into the air, encircling my head with trails of smoke. As the ashen scent settles onto my clothes, I hold the bundle out to each of the four winds and say a prayer to each. When the prayers are said, I sprinkle ash from the burned sage onto the grinding stone. Using the fist-sized stone again, I return to the shards.

The crackle of shards is bone crunching and the rasp of pottery against stone is the moan of Those Gone Before. Then I tell a new story, of the return of old spirits and the departure of new ones. As I sing the Acoma prayer of peace again, an even older prayer comes to my lips and I sing it loudly as the pottery reduces to a fine, russet powder. I run my fingers through the powder, feeling the dormant currents of life awaiting release. Mingled in them, I feel my daughter's spirit and she whispers her story to me. It is so short, but it's enough.

The currents blend into a solid strand and I feel its strength mounting. Wanting Mansi to know her father's story, I slip my wedding ring from my finger and lay it in the powder. This ring is my closest tie to Hanu.

Inhaling deeply, I grab a pointed shard from the dust and slice it across my left palm. Blood rushes up from the gash as I press my hand into the powder. I wince, the russet brightening to a rich sienna as the powder congeals into paste. I sing of the Sky City, sandstone mesas, and stone formations—and the Great Star Nation beyond them until the powder and my blood are one. My life force merges with those awakening. Fighting for control, I say the words again. I hold my palm up to the burnt orange sky and chant to

Mansi and Those Gone Before. For Mansi and Hanu—and me—I tell them the old stories and the new as I mix life and stillness.

The paste gleams until streams of white light rise from the desert floor. The light wraps around my ankles and coils around my body until it slips through my arm and into the paste. The biosphere trembles. My body shudders. The paste pulsates until a thrum of whispers—of Those Gone Before—fills the expanse.

They have awakened.

The ruddy sky erupts with white light. It undulates on the horizon and across the desert floor. The light envelops me. I gasp as a new story spills from my mouth. These words are in a language I've never known, but I feel the words in my bones. I hear them in my soul.

My abdomen aches again. I slide my hand beneath my shirt and streak pasty stripes across my still-swollen abdomen. Then I whisper a prayer for healing. The paste pulsates white with ancient energy as it sinks into my flesh. The pain deepens, blinding and sharp, until it pierces my abdomen. I double over, feeling my life force intertwine and then separate with the ancient energy.

The sky flashes with an arc of brilliant white light and then the white light vanishes.

I lay my hand against Mansi's grave. This time, all I feel is stillness. I lay my hands against the ground, feeling the shards. No restless currents of life eddy against my palms.

It is done.

Another pain presses into my abdomen. Surprised, I jerk my hand toward the pain and heat radiates against my palm. I feel the stirring of life inside me.

I rise to my feet and pull my wedding ring from the drying paste. After cleaning it on my shirttail, I put it back on my finger. When I feel steady enough, I pick up my satchel and walk back to the house.

It is night when Hanu returns home. He pauses beside the dining table. Only a small counter separates the dining table from the kitchen where I prepare the last of our supper. The door onto the deck is open, letting in the warm air. From the table, we can see the deck and our desert property beyond. I step around Hanu and set a bowl of potatoes on the table beside the salad and cooked fish.

Hanu's face is smeared with dirt and he has already shed his environmental suit. He steps into the kitchen, looking uncomfortable, lost. He has been lost for a very long time. He studies me for a moment and then the hint of a smile touches his lips.

"'Sovi, . . . I'm sorry about this morning. I was wrong to be so demanding."

"It's all right, Hanu," I say and move toward the kitchen.

He follows me, pausing at the sink to wash his hands and face. He dries them on a towel as I pick up a basket of bread and then he follows to the table. I set down the bread.

"'Sovi, I—"

Finally, he reaches for me and I put my arms around him. At last, the distance retreats and I feel him sag. "I love you, 'Sovi. I would never leave you behind. I'm so sorry for saying that."

I smile, surprised by his unusual flexibility. Hanu has always rigidly made up his mind. "I know. I love you, Hanu."

"I feel so lost, 'Sovi. Help me."

I hold him tighter. I can help him find his way now. "It's all right. We'll find the path again."

After a moment, he lets go of me and collapses into a chair. I slide my arms around his neck and kiss him gently. His cedary scent is comforting.

"But, 'Sovi—this place. I can't go back to Earth without you, but my spirit is dying in this place."

I drop down beside him and his gaze meets mine. "For you, I will go." It will be best for the child that I carry. I will tell him soon. It will be best for him, too, so he can reclaim his Acoma heritage and learn how important it will be for the colony's survival.

His mouth gapes and he stares at me, unblinking, for a moment. "You will return with me?" He holds his breath.

I nod. "All I ask is that you wait three months."

He laughs, relief spilling from his voice. "Yes, anything as long as you are with me!"

He pulls me into his arms again and his lips press urgently

against mine. His breath is warm against my neck, his hands caressing. His walnut hair is soft against my cheek. Exhausted, I lay my head against his shoulder.

Every day that passes, I feel the warmth of life inside me, eagerly filling the emptiness. As I gaze out at the biosphere, I touch the hand-painted pottery beads around my neck. I formed them from the tempered paste. The beads sparkle at my touch. This new child, only partly ours, carries some of the life force brought back from the shards. And a bit of Mansi's life force, too. When this child arrives, she will carry the knowledge and memories of Those Gone Before, but she will learn the Acoma ways, too.

Casting one last look at the desert landscape, I slip into my environmental suit. Everything has been packed and sent to the nearby transport pad. I won't miss the biospheres, but we will return here some day to show our daughter the rest of her heritage.

Hanu carries the last of our bags through the airlock. When he returns, his smile radiates a peace I have not seen in a long while.

"Are you ready, 'Sovi?" he asks, adjusting a strap on his environmental suit.

"Almost." I take hold of his hand. "There is something I need to tell you."

He frowns, a wary look in his eyes. "You haven't changed your mind, have you?"

I lean against him and whisper in his ear. "You are going to be a father again."

"A father? But Dr. Jeffries said—" A sob escapes his lips. "Are you sure?"

I nod. I am certain.

"And you are still willing to go back to Earth?" His eyes are wide.

"No," I say, laying a finger to his lips. "I am willing to go *with* you. I want our daughter to know the Acoma pueblo as well as the Martian landscape. Will you return with me when our daughter is old enough to travel here?"

He thinks for a moment then nods. "I will follow you anywhere, Chasovi." Then he grins. "A father."

Soon, I will tell him about his daughter and Those Gone Before, for their life forces are forever intertwined and inseparable. Through our daughter, Mars will one day awaken its old ways. All Those Gone Before ever wanted was to walk these red sands again, to bring life to their dead homeworld. Our daughter will know their history and their lost language as well as the dying Keresan tongue. Maybe through her, she can preserve them both?

With his arm around my waist, Hanu and I step out of the airlock.

Through our daughter, all the Martian glyphs will be read and understood. Maybe then, the entire Mars colony will learn how we can leave our sterile biospheres and walk the red sands without environmental suits. That might be enough to bring all of Those Gone Before home again.

A UNIVERSAL SPECTRUM

I never noticed all the colors in a prism until I heard Johnny was dying.

But standing here at Lime Kiln Point, the sharp wind in my face and the lighthouse at my back, I see the full spectrum. The prism Johnny gave me feels cold against my fingers now, like his hands in the hospital growing colder with the moments, like my father's glare at the funeral as I passed him without speaking.

Colors reflect against my jacket from an unstable moment of Haro Strait sunlight. The sea smells crisp like a rain-soaked sheet and the tang of pine cones infuses the air, covering the lingering scent of antiseptic and mums. Sunset approaches. Johnny and I shared a lot of summer nights together, catching frogs, playing kick-the-can, and hiding secrets that children should never keep.

This is the only thing he's ever asked of me, so I'll stay here as long as it takes. For Johnny.

I clutch the prism tighter and wait for the signs. The weather report says it will be too cloudy to see the lunar eclipse or the comet, but Johnny says—said—I will. (It's so hard to think of him in past tense now.) Either way, it will be a long night.

The last ten years ebb and flow against the rocks as the sun slips closer to the white-capped Olympic Mountains. One last time, here on Haro Strait, I'll return to my past.

Streetlights pooled across rain-damp streets, the scent of burning grass husky in the cool air. Stars winked in the indigo darkness, crickets and cicadas scritching. The clackety clack of bicycles—and laughter—echoed through the screen of my bedroom window. Voices rose and fell beneath the old apple tree as a metallic clank bounced through the night.

They were setting up for kick-the-can. I'd never made it far enough to kick that can, but hearing it strike the ground filled me with excitement. Feet pounded damp ground. A shriek pealed into laughter. Whispers carried sharply on the wind.

I sat at my desk doing my fifth grade homework, wanting desperately to be with them, playing kick-the-can, but not until the algebra was finished. Below my bedroom, the dull murmur of the television resonated. I could almost feel its hum in the wooden floor against my stocking feet. For a few moments, water surged in the kitchen and fell silent. Mom was finishing the dishes.

Giggles and clanging rang out. I glanced through the screen, the night cool and inviting, the scent of burning grass and charcoal strong. I grinned. Someone had reached home and kicked the can.

A car door slammed, the sound like gun fire.

I lurched in my chair and the trembling began, the fear old and dark like the burnt out heaps of field grass left beside the curb. Daddy was home.

He clomped through the back doorway, his voice throbbing through the house. My room felt cold as I gripped the edge of my three-ring binder. Shaking, I hurried to my closet, climbing inside. Fabric softener mixed with baby powder and lavender sachet. Shoes lined the closet bottom—dress shoes my older sister gave me that I couldn't wear yet. I wasn't old enough to wear heels. Someday these would go to my younger sister, Betsy, but I hoped not.

Dresses and pants hung like curtains in the half-darkness and I wished I could hide in their pressed folds. I drew my knees against my heaving chest and afraid to move, I listened for the creak of boots on the stairs. So soft the sound, so secret.

The television blared below now, canned laughter overshadowing the happy voices outside.

In a short time, the creaks moaned through the house and I

pressed my hands to my ears. Why couldn't Mom hear those creaks? Why couldn't she hear the boots on the stairs, the heavy work boots that walked those stairs without anyone knowing, without anyone telling?

My door whined open. Sickening sweet after-shave and the musty scent of seawater clung to his clothes as he stood in front of the closet, his work boots mildewy and his voice husky. I pinched my eyes closed. His lean frame shadowed the high heels and his heavy breath filled the room. Why couldn't Mom hear his boots above her?

"Dana," he cooed. "Where's daddy's girl?"

Cold fear washed over me. Trembling, I concentrated on the children's voices outside. I felt so cut off from them. So different. I didn't ever want to be daddy's girl again.

His stubbled, too-tanned face peered into the closet, his eyes burning.

His clammy hands slid down my arms, pulling me from the closet. Tears funneled down my hot cheeks. My limbs were frozen with fear, unable to shove him away. He pulled me against him. His hot breath was sour, ragged, his face and hands rough.

"Is that any way to greet your Daddy?"

My stomach churned as he pressed himself against me. His hands touched me in ways I didn't understand.

Below me, my mother and little sister talked. Television murmured. Wooden floor creaked. Outside, faraway children laughed. Inside, I cried.

When he left me, disheveled and sobbing, I stripped away every trace of him, washing and washing in the bathroom sink until my skin chafed and puckered. I put on my sweat suit. Then I climbed out my window, crept across the roof, and climbed into the apple tree. The smoky June silence and the rusty, dented remnants of kick-the-can lay beneath the tree as I climbed down. I huddled in the tree's dark safety, hidden from the glare of the security light, and wept.

"Don't cry," came a warm, innocent voice.

"Who's there," I called, my voice raw and hoarse.

A dark-haired boy with a sweet smile and bright blue eyes stepped from the darkness. "I'm Johnny," he said. "Is the game over?" He peered at me, moving closer. "Why are you crying?"

I hid my face. I couldn't say the words. I couldn't even think them.

He sat down beside me in the dirt and gently laid his hand against my arm. At first, I flinched, but his touch was so comforting.

"I know now," he said, his voice nothing but softness. "How long has he—"

Horrified, I gaped at him. "Please, you can't tell!"

Crickets chirred. Leaves rustled. Wind whispered through branches.

Johnny glanced toward the security light and frowned. "It's so bright." He held his hand up, covering the light with his palm. Almost instantly, the glaring light blinked out. Silvery darkness filled the backyard as he drew his hand against his side. It was so strange, yet so wondrous.

He turned and grinned. "You can't tell about me either, okay?"

I nodded. "Where do you come from?"

"The beginning," he said. "And I'll be here to the end, to understand, to become."

I didn't understand a word he said, but his presence was comforting. He reached out for my hand and something cool pressed against my palm. It gleamed brighter than the now-dark security light.

"What is it?"

Johnny was silent for a moment. "A sun catcher," he said finally. "It holds in light. It'll protect you. Someday, I'll ask you to give it back to me."

As the winds rose, carrying smoke and summer aloft, I heard the future in his voice. Johnny wouldn't be here long, but he'd always be my friend. And the secrets we'd shared would be kept—at least his would.

I draw a long, steady breath, surfacing from the past, and step across the rocky shore. The lighthouse isn't far. Johnny asked me to come here after the funeral. (He didn't have any family, so I paid for the meager service with a student loan.) My stomach aches at the memory of his boyish face, all stillness and pasty, his lids stiff against those bright blue eyes, the sweet grin molded into an unnatural final expression. I shove away the image. That wasn't Johnny. Johnny was laughter and wonder.

I lay the round, faceted sun catcher against my cheek, but it remains cold as it reflects soft colors against the rocks. I feel Johnny so close again, like I always did when I held the sun catcher as a child. I feel the gentle, comforting touch of his fingers against my arm.

The sun peeks through the cottony swath of clouds again and the water glitters teal, frothy caps gleaming pale mint. Delicate black fins churn playfully past the point. Harbor porpoises. Clouds skim the horizon, shielding the mountains. The sun won't last long. My heart is heavy, but my spirit stirs. This place has a way of getting into my bones. I feel Johnny's presence here. Again, I dip a hand into my past.

As he did every night, Johnny waited for me beneath the apple tree. He didn't go to school, but he wanted to learn, to be like the other children. So did I. He wasn't like anyone I'd ever known and even now, an explanation escaped me. Under the silvery glow of that strange light, I taught him from my school books and he gave me courage.

I carried the sun catcher in my pocket and kept it beside my bed when I slept. At night, when the lights were out, it pulsed with a faint silvery gleam. During the day, it had a silver afterglow as if gathering the sunshine. Slowly, at first, Daddy left me alone. I remembered many a night, I sat in my closet clutching the sun catcher to my chest, trying to block its glow. I held my breath when Daddy peeked beneath the dresses and pants. Whenever I held the sun catcher, his gaze passed through me—as if I were invisible. Once he left my room, I hurried out my window to the backyard where I laughed and read with Johnny.

He smiled at me one evening as he looked up from his book. "It seems such a long time here," he said. "I envy you that."

I frowned at him and pressed the sun catcher against my cheek. His eyes closed for a moment, almost as if I'd caressed his cheek with my hand. "What do you mean?"

"You grow up, you grow old, the years building. You have so much time to become wise, to pass on what you know, what you've learned." He sighed. "You have so much time."

Back then, I thought we had forever. We had so many summers left to chase the stars. If only I'd known how few Johnny had.

"You do too," I said.

His gaze fell to the sun catcher. "I have as long as the sun allows," he answered. His eyes narrowed. "But you, you have a long time. Don't let him steal all of it away from you."

I bristled. "You promised not to talk about that."

"No, I promised not to tell," he corrected me gently. "And I won't, but you must, Dana."

I shook my head, the fear hard in my stomach. "You said the sun catcher would protect me! It hides me from him."

He squinted at the prism. "It doesn't hide you. Look at it again. In time, you'll see it. Then you'll know what to do."

I started to ask him to explain, but the neighborhood kids rushed into the backyard with a shiny new can.

"Dana, wanna play?" Sheila, a fourth grader from down the lane, asked. Her ponytail was tight against her scalp and she wore a blue windbreaker, her cheeks puffy and red from running.

"Can Johnny play too?"

"Sure," said Sheila. "He can even set up the can." She extended the new can to Johnny.

His face gleamed almost silver, his eyes wide, his mouth gaping, as he reached gingerly for the old Folger's can. He held it as if it were the most wondrous thing he'd ever touched. With reverence, he positioned it in the dirt beneath the apple tree. More children hurried into the backyard and a keeper was chosen. The keeper began to count, his squeaky voice piercing in the calm night air. I took hold of Johnny's hot hand and pulled him toward the street, around the house. The warmth from his hand traveled up my arm, into my shoulder and across my chest. We kept running until we reached the field next door.

Streetlights were stark against the tall grasses that swished against our calves. Johnny and I ducked down, waiting to circle around toward the backyard. One by one, the neighborhood kids were captured by the keeper. Feet pounded against hard ground. Voices whispered. A car chugged by, the sound fading into the night. We kept low against the fence as we rushed through the shadows toward the security light illuminating that can.

The keeper was near the can when Johnny and I slipped over the fence. Taking a deep breath, I ran into the light, luring the keeper toward me. As I felt his breath against my neck, the dull clang of a can striking the ground rang out. I stopped running and turned. There he stood, ghost pale in the glare of the security light, his arms thrust toward the sky. He shouted unintelligibly as he danced around the can. The newly released captives bounced around beside him, cheering him. Johnny was so proud. I envied him that moment.

Sunlight slips back through the clouds as I step away from my childhood, but a touch of warmth lingers in my palm—only for a moment. I remember how Johnny's hands felt that night. Warm, loving. Not like those awful touches that still haunt me sometimes late at night in the darkness.

The ground is level near the lighthouse, so I spread out my blanket and sit. Moonrise is a few hours off. I turn the prism over and over in my hand. Over the years, I've thought it so many things. I thought it bent light to create illusions, to fool Daddy into not seeing me . . . to fool myself into keeping silent. Later, I thought it colored over the secrets, making them not so bad somehow.

I didn't understand until Daddy walked past my room and into Betsy's.

My chest ached, the fear wild inside me as I concentrated on the prism's warm glow, gathering my courage, and hurried into the hall. Fighting down my fear, I sucked in a breath and shoved open my little sister's door. Betsy cried silently, Daddy's hands on her arms, her nightgown unbuttoned.

"No! I won't let you do it!"

He tried to silence me, but I stomped my feet on the floor and shrieked. He rushed at me, fury in his eyes, hand raised to strike me. I stuck out my chin to him, daring him. He couldn't hurt me anymore.

The prism's light spilled onto the wooden floor in animated spheres. Then Mom was at the door. Horrified, she shoved past Daddy, gathering me against her as she moved toward Betsy.

"Get out of this house," said Mom, her voice pinched, her gaze murderous.

Daddy opened his mouth to protest, but Mom snapped a finger toward the door. He turned without a word and fled.

I told Mom everything that night. She cried and held me. When she had composed herself and calmed Betsy, she phoned my older sister. And more painful truth followed. Then the police.

I let the old pain go, reaching instead for the raw hurt of losing Johnny.

Night has slipped across the strait, spring stars spilling across the sky. Fir trees silhouette the horizon, a ship's call mournful in the stillness. Pacific waters dance across the rocks.

The time drags by and I know Johnny would have enjoyed that slowness. At last, the moon rises over the water. In a short time, a shadow begins to press across the face of the moon. The water sparkles, the waves glowing green against the rocks. I grin. It's a brightness much stronger than phytoplankton release.

I search the sky until I see the tail of a comet stretching through the darkness.

Abruptly, a low hum filters into the calm. I glance down. The sun catcher. It gleams brighter than the lighthouse's beacon. I lean toward the sun catcher, bringing it closer to my ear.

There is no sound, but I hear voices. My ten-year-old voice sobbing, Johnny's gentle voice comforting me. The events of ten years filter backward through the prism until I hear where he comes from. I stare at the stars sprinkled across the darkness. His home is out there somewhere. He knew he could never return. Our world—our sun—made his time so short, but his time is invaluable to his people.

Sometimes, I think he braved it just for me.

I press the prism against my ear, smiling. It's been a long time in their years since they have translated our universal greeting. Johnny came here looking human to learn about us, to understand us. Our life-giving star his doom.

It's all so fragile, isn't it?

The sun catcher was his record, his truth of learning to become human. Through him, I learned how, too.

I rise stiffly from the ground and hold my arm up to the sky—like Johnny told me to do. The prism pulsates in my hand, growing so bright I have to shield my eyes. In an instant, the sun catcher shoots from my palm and across the sky, under the cover of the comet. I watch it rise and wink out into the darkness. It leaves a purple after-image in the sky that lingers for a moment.

It's done, Johnny. I've sent your record home.

I sit down on the blanket and watch the boats drift past, listening to the lighthouse's melancholy call. I wonder how Johnny's people will interpret his records and I hope that one day soon we'll hear a universal reply from some distant place. Until then, I will think of Johnny and thank him for the spectrum of years that stretch before me.

PEACE OF LACE

The sun sank low behind the trees, turning the umber gravel road that led out of the cemetery into a coppery ribbon. The attendants had finished with the grave site hours ago, leaving only a mound of red earth and eight bouquets of flowers to catch the final rays of sunlight before nightfall. Samantha paused near her car on the gravel road and stared at her guitar case in the back seat. She did not want to approach that cold gravestone or her three sisters clustered around the floral sprays.

She hadn't seen her sisters in four years. Time had a way of twisting arguments until no one remembered why they had begun or how to resolve them. Not even Aunt Mabel, the family peace-maker, could untie this knot. Sam twisted the piece of lace on her keychain around her index finger. Aunt Mabel had been one of the last lace makers in Ballard County. This sturdy strand of ivory lace reminded Sam of a snowflake. Sam's initials were woven into the top. Aunt Mabel had given it to her as a hair ribbon, but Sam never grew her auburn hair long enough to use it. Instead, she tied it to her keychain. Aunt Mabel had always said that the beauty of lace came from the many threads woven together to create endless patterns. And the magic of lace lay in that pattern. Most of the family thought she was crazy. Cece, Sam's oldest sister, thought she was a witch, but Sam had found Aunt Mabel's ways healing.

Sam watched Cece cup a hand over her eyes and watch her

approach. No doubt waiting for her to stagger. Cece's face scrunched, her lips stretching into a taut arc, and then she turned away. Annette, the second oldest stood with bowed head beside a pink bouquet of carnations. She turned her head a fraction to gaze over at Sam, but when their gaze met, she turned her eyes downward. Nikki, the youngest, tossed back her shoulder length, chestnut hair and smiled. Nikki. She had been too young to understand the yelling, the door slamming and the blackouts, just like she'd been too young to understand why Mom had left them.

Horrible scenes from Cece's wedding reception rushed back to Sam. She vaguely remembered that her date, a guy that she'd met the night before, wore a leather jacket to the reception which sent Cece into a rage. All four of them ended up in a shouting match followed by four years of silence. Over a crude guy in a leather jacket? Was there anything sillier?

She sighed and gazed across the country field with its neatly aligned headstones. Everything in perfect order, even the dead. Aunt Mabel used to say there was a place for everything. The symmetry of these stones would have pleased her—this feud would not. It wasn't about that guy in the leather jacket. It was about the downhill slide that Sam had been on, drinking too much and hanging out in bars until they closed. That guy, whose name she had long forgotten, represented that lifestyle and Cece had wanted no part of that for Sam or for herself. Sam sighed. Aunt Mabel had said to apologize and put that reception behind them, but that was something Sam could never do. To apologize for that guy was to apologize for her life. Too bad Aunt Mabel would never see the resolution.

Guess there was no more stalling, Sam decided, and straightened her navy suit jacket. She couldn't avoid her sisters any longer. Her heels sank into the soft ground as she stepped down toward the grave. She wondered if her wavering steps made her appear drunk—no doubt a familiar sight to them. Her shadow rushed on ahead, falling across the mound of earth, and she wanted to pull it back, to slow down time so she would not have to face them. She gripped the lace on her keychain tighter, feeling the coarse threads digging into her hand. It sent warmth streaking through her fingers. She didn't want to say good-bye and she didn't want to say she was sorry. Two of the most painful yet simple tasks, requiring only a couple of words.

Tears stung her dry eyes at the sight of the flowers. All through the showing and the funeral, she felt numb, tears flowing, but the realization hovered nearby. Aunt Mabel was really gone, leaving the broken, scattered pieces of her nieces' lives—lives she'd always tried to stitch back together. Sam clutched the lace tighter. Aunt Mabel had never married. It was whispered sometimes at family reunions that she had been engaged once, to a soldier, but he was killed in action. Soon after, she buried herself in her sewing and that's when her fascination with lace had begun.

Sam remembered the sleek walnut bobbins lying in a neat row on the green velvet pillow. She had tried to teach Sam how to make the lace, but Sam never could handle all the bobbins, nevermind master the patterns that Aunt Mabel knew by rote. She never needed those paper grid patterns that had made Sam's eyes cross. All the intertwining threads were too much—too much to keep track of, yet there was a sort of—music about the bobbin lace.

How the bobbins clicked as she twisted pairs of silky threads around and through each other, zzzl-hum, zzzl-hum, reminding her almost of a soft drum beat that would stay with her long after the cramps left her fingers. At first, she had embraced the melody, trying to recreate it on the guitar, but it quickly became too much for her, along with everything else in her life. There was such power in that music that grew so strong she had to escape it. Soon after, she gave up the guitar and that strange melody for a bottle of vodka. She wanted peace. It was only when she got the phone call that Aunt Mabel had passed away that she thought about playing the guitar again. The music of those bobbins would be a healing song to her now.

A hand touched her arm. Cece. She glanced up at Cece's tear-streaked face and noticed the lace tucked into her lapel pocket. It seemed to shimmer in the fading sunlight.

"I can't believe she's gone," Cece whispered.

Sam pointed at her lapel pocket. "Did she make that?"

Cece nodded. She reached up and yanked out the lace. The stark white threads created a series of blocks and eyelets that ended with the letters 'CJC.' "Don't know why, but wearing it made me feel better."

Sam smiled, blinking back tears, and held out her keychain. "I know." She felt the rhythmic beat of her pulse throbbing down into her fingertips.

Annette leaned over to Sam and pointed to the pink lace that she had coiled around her silver watch band. Sam noticed the block letters 'ARC' at the top of the lace strand. "She gave this to me last year and told me not to lose it."

Nikki, holding out a lavender envelope, stepped over to Sam and squeezed her hand. "Aunt Mabel sent this letter to me last month with a piece of lace in it. She told me not to lose it—that I should give it to you."

From the envelope, Nikki removed a long strip of lavender lace and Sam took it. There at the top were Nikki's initials, 'NMC.'

"Why give it to me?"

Nikki shook her head. She reached into the envelope and in her hand was a slender walnut bobbin. "She said I should give you this too. She said it belonged to her mother."

"What's that?" Annette asked. She brushed her mahogany hair off her forehead and tilted her head out of the sunlight.

Sam smiled. "A bobbin."

She reached gently toward the bobbin and took it in her palm. Instantly, the beat of a bodhrain drum echoed through her head overlaid with the zzzl-hum of the bobbins clicking in Aunt Mabel's hand. At first, it startled her and she drew back from the music. But it was wonderful. It made her adrenalin pump and her spirits soar. Suddenly, she realized that she and her sisters were talking. They had talked! She tried to find some words to fill the silence that pressed down on them like an anvil when something glinted and her gaze darted toward the light. A silver spark winked at her and spiraled through the white lace, tracing up and over until it disappeared. Suddenly, she needed to talk—to explain.

"I know we haven't spoken in a long time," Sam began, feeling her throat tighten. "I know now that I shouldn't have brought that guy to your reception, Cece."

"It doesn't matter now, Sam," Cece answered. "In your condition, you didn't know what you were doing?"

Silence hovered around them for a long while until Sam saw a silver spark dance across the lace in Cece's pocket. The music swelled around Sam and for an instant, she imagined herself on a hillside, ancient drums beating in a circle around her.

"You're right," Sam said finally. "I—I had a terrible drinking problem back then. I know that now, but I'm recovering. Anyway, I just wanted to say—I was sorry."

Cece's jaw line sharpened. "But are you serious about trying to recover?"

"I haven't drank in a year."

"That's good to hear, Samantha."

"You were out of control back then," Annette added. "You just couldn't see it. But Aunt Mabel saw it."

Sam sighed. She was the only one who hadn't said a word either. Aunt Mabel had acted like nothing had happened the next day. Didn't even attempt a lecture, not that Sam had been sober enough to have heard it. Shortly after that, she had made Sam that piece of lace, telling her that when she understood the pattern, everything would be okay. Sam gazed down at her strand of ivory lace, seeing the same half moons and teardrops she had seen four years ago. Within the multitude of strands were four strands of silver thread wound together to make the pattern. Four strands. She wanted to laugh out loud. It was so simple, but not back then to an alcoholic who chose to drown out the music—her own music. Aunt Mabel knew it was healing magic that she wove into her lace and she didn't want that healing magic to die with her, but Sam hadn't understood that until now.

"I know," Sam said finally. "And I'm sorry for that too."

Annette slipped her arm around Sam's waist. "Glad to hear it."

Sam glanced at the lace surrounding Annette's watch and pulled it free.

"What are you doing?"

"I know what to do now," Sam said. "Cece, give me your lace."

Cece frowned. "Why?"

"It's important."

Cece plucked the lace from her pocket and laid it in Sam's hand. Sam tied Annette and Cece's strands together. After untying her strand from the keychain, she tied it to Annette's strand.

"Nik, give me yours."

Nikki held out the lavender lace and Sam tied it to the end of her strand. As she wrapped the other end of the lavender over the crisp white of Cece's lace, she noticed more initials on the lavender strand, 'CASN.' The first letter of each of their names. She swallowed a sob as she tied the ends together, forming a lace wreath. Symmetry. Suddenly a pulse of silver light traced over the strands, spiraled up like an apparition into the approaching twilight and vanished. Everything had its place and as she'd always done, Aunt Mabel had put even these pieces back in place. There before Sam, outlined in silver thread, was an intricate pattern of Celtic knot work.

Cece reached out and hugged her. "I'm sorry, Sam," she said. "I gave up on you."

"So did I," Sam whispered.

When Cece let go of her, Sam turned back to Aunt Mabel's grave. Everything in its place, she thought and laid the lace wreath on Aunt Mabel's grave. Like Aunt Mabel, she had the patterns in her head now and some day, she hoped to teach them to her sisters.

SURVIVING THE ELEPHANT

Death hissed across the smoke-laden cornfield, percussion shells thundering against the damp, loamy soil. With shaking hands, Private Tim Adams of the 14th Massachusetts Volunteer Rifle regiment clung to his Springfield rifle as he fumbled to reload it. Minié balls sizzled past his head and thumped against the dirt, the ground quaking beneath him. Parrott guns roared overhead, the Federal battery blasting away at the Rebs who rained molten lead on him and the other soldiers. The farm fields of Sharpsburg, Maryland swarmed with blue and gray and Tim longed for the safety of his bedroll. Anything to escape this hailstorm of musket balls and percussion shells!

Last night's cool rains had swirled thick, early morning fog across the fields. That shroud had concealed him and the others among the cornstalks, but now, the autumn sun burned it away, leaving the air heavy and muggy. Ahead, in the roiling battle smoke, butternut and gray uniforms flashed among the tall, dry cornstalks.

The regiment of fifty had never been in combat before—they'd never "seen the elephant" as the seasoned soldiers called it. It meant living through some of the worst moments life had to throw at you. Captain Benjamin Adams, Tim's Pa, had seen the elephant in the Mexican war—so had his oldest brother, Chris. And it killed him, too. Soon after, Captain Adams dismissed Tim from the regiment, on account of him being the only surviving son, but Tim had come to Sharpsburg anyway. He'd prove to his Pa that he could survive the elephant. And he'd make sure that his Pa came home.

The 14th Massachusetts had orders to route the Rebs in Mumma's swale, a low, swampy tract of land below, but the Rebs weren't ready to give up this cornfield yet or anything beyond it.

A minié ball snicked past Tim's face. He fell to his stomach, the dirt slick and smelling of blood, and steadied his rifle on a shattered cornstalk. Rod McIntyre and Avery Simms lay beside him, loading their Springfields. His father crouched several feet ahead at the front of the regiment, unaware that Tim had slipped into the line just east of Antietam creek. Some of the other New England regiments crouched beside them. So many men had fallen this day, and night was still a few hours away.

Wave after wave of rifle fire cut through the sprawling cornfield, scattering tall, dried stalks and ears of Indian corn. Like the swing of Death's scythe, the Rebs' intense fire cut down everything in its path. Clouds of hot, sulfury smoke hung over the field, choking Tim with heat and stench. His throat was raw, his canteen empty. Powder clung to his face and chafed his flesh as he huddled against the thin stalks.

In front of him, a man shuddered and fell to the ground, pierced by a bullet. Another man on Avery's right slumped dead. Avery panicked and struggled to his feet, but Tim grabbed his arm and jerked him down. Avery's chin smashed against the dirt.

"Stay down!" Tim shouted. Avery and Rod sprawled against the rich soil, white-knuckling their Springfields.

The roar of muskets was constant, punctuated by the pounding of percussion shells and Federal canisters. Tim and the others returned fire, yet the flashes of butternut and gray slipped closer through the corn like ghosts.

Frantically, Tim dug out a cartridge from his haversack, tore it, and rammed it into the rifle's muzzle. He dug through his haversack again, to count his cartridges, when his fingers closed around a smooth object. He pulled it out. Chris's pocket watch!

The watch had belonged to their great grandfather and passed down four generations. Pa had given it to Chris when he enlisted, telling him the watch had a magic to it, but Chris hadn't wanted to harm the watch. He rarely carried it into battle. When Chris's things were sent home, the watch had been sent to Tim with a letter. It had only been a few lines, scrawled in an army hospital, but they still choked Tim up. *Keep this watch close to your heart, Tim, and I'll always be with you.* For a moment, Tim stared at the faded gold casing with its dented backing and slid the pocket watch into his left breast pocket.

The fighting had gone on for hours of unending slaughter. Weary, aching, and sick of the carnage, Tim faced yet another endless charge by the Rebs. Would it ever end? Would he ever see Massachusetts again or his Ma? He'd seen so much death today. Why had so many died? No matter how many fell, the Rebs kept surging forward, holding the cornfield's southern boundaries.

"They just keep comin'!" shouted Rod, a brown-haired, nine-teen-year-old soldier. He was a Concord boy like Tim, only a year older, too. They became good friends since he signed on four months ago. "When they gonna stop?"

A wry smile touched Avery's bloodied, bruised face as he fired through the cornfield. He brushed powder out of his wavy, blond hair. His face was reddened from the sun and smudged with dirt and blood. "When the devil himself waves a white flag."

"Forward, men! Charge!" Captain Adams commanded. It swelled above the battle roar. "Let's run them out of here!"

"Pa must have spied the devil's flag then!" Tim shouted. "Move out! They're runnin'!"

Tim and his comrades scrambled to their feet and rushed through Mumma's cornfield, rifles smoking. They tumbled out of the corn-field amidst a shower of nearby canister that nearly deafened them. The Rebs had scrambled toward the west woods, butternut and gray uniforms torn and bloodied. As the last man disappeared into its smoking boughs, a hail of minié balls careened out of the west woods. Ahead, on the edge of a meadow near the farm lane, lay some large rocks.

"Flank left!" shouted Captain Adams who surged toward the rise above the farm lane.

Tim and the others swarmed toward the rocks, grateful for any cover in this open terrain.

"I'm hit!" shouted Avery, dropping to the ground.

Tim grabbed him by the arms and dragged him down to the rocks. Rod stopped to help another soldier out of the cornfield and down to the rocks. Tim collapsed beside Avery and hurriedly opened the young man's coat collar. A minié ball had lodged against his collarbone. Tim slipped a handkerchief out of his pocket and pressed it to the wound. It was all he could do, but Avery would be okay.

"Hold this against the wound to stop the bleeding. Okay?"

Avery was panting wildly, his eyes squeezed closed. Finally, he nodded. Tim grabbed Avery's canteen from his belt and pressed it to the blond soldier's lips. Avery drank a mouthful and then pushed the canteen back. "Not much left."

Tim understood. His own canteen was empty. He longed to take a drink of Avery's water, but Avery needed it more than he did. He closed the canteen and slipped it back onto Avery's belt.

Confederate snipers continued to fire at them from the west woods. They were reforming their units—Tim could feel it. His heart hammered against his chest. The Rebs wouldn't let them hold Mumma's cornfield for long. They hadn't all morning.

Tim glanced over at his pa, Captain Adams. He crouched with four regiment officers behind the boulders. Pa was a slim, stately man with dark hair, kind eyes, and a thin moustache that framed his mouth. Pa looked as battle weary as the rest of his officers, but in those kind eyes, Tim saw command weighing heavy. Tim felt guilty now. His being here would only add to Pa's burden. If Lee's army moved north, then Chris and his entire regiment died for nothing. Jaw set, fingers taut against his Springfield, Tim patted the pocket watch. For Chris, he'd gaze upon the elephant and help hold back the Rebs.

A percussion shell shrieked overhead from a Confederate battery in the west woods and slammed into the cornfield only a few hundred feet behind them. The impact knocked them to the ground, scattering cornstalks in its wake. Tim was nearly knocked unconscious. He held on as the smoky, roaring landscape spun around him. His rifle clattered against the rocks and fell into the grass.

Rod retrieved the fallen rifle and pressed it into Tim's hands. "You okay?" He pulled the dazed young man back against the rocks.

Tim nodded, his head still ringing. "That was a close one."

"Closer than I'd like."

Rod pointed south toward the haystacks and barn where a concentration of Confeds had gathered. They were aiming at one of the Federal batteries above Mumma's swale. They were also pinning down Tim's regiment, preventing them from advancing onto the bloody farm lane below where so many soldiers already lay dead. Tim turned his gaze from the lane, his heart sick.

"They're giving our artillery hell up there," said Tim.

Nodding, Rod reloaded his rifle and fired toward the haystacks. His shot caught a gray uniform.

Tim fired off a shot across the smoky terrain beyond the farm lane and reloaded. He didn't want to know if he'd hit anything or not.

Tim and the rest of the 14th Massachusetts Volunteers continued to hold position, firing off shots at the snipers near Piper's barn. Pa seemed restless. He crouched low, traversing the cluster of rocks as he checked on his men. Tim ducked his head before his pa passed him with only a quick tap on the sleeve. He glanced up after his Pa had slipped past. On both sides, wounded soldiers were being tended. Tim reached over to Avery and gently touched his sleeve.

"You okay, Avery?"

"Yeah," he said with a crooked smile. "They haven't done me in yet."

The sniper fire concentrated on the battery above Tim's regiment. To Tim's relief, the shooting was tapering off. Maybe the Rebs were out of ammunition? His pa leaned against the rocks, seemingly relieved at the lengthening moments of quiet. There hadn't been any all day. The sun was starting a slow slide out of the sky and Tim prayed they'd all be alive at sundown.

Digging through his haversack, Tim opened his cartridge box, tore a cartridge, and reloaded his Springfield. Then he slid the old pocket watch out of his pocket. Despite its battered, worn appearance, the watch had always kept perfect time. The sun hung low, at least four o'clock. He checked the watch. It was almost five o'clock. Thankfully, darkness would fall early. The watch felt warm and soothing in his hand, as if his brother's arm had slid around his shoulders. He forgot about his thirst and the aches in his muscles. The emptiness in his stomach eased and a calm filled him.

The hand clamping onto his shoulder startled him. He whirled, staring into his father's weary, angry gaze.

"Tim! What in blazes!" Pa grabbed him by the shoulders, fear slipping past his anger.

"Pa, I had to come! For Chris." He squeezed Pa's arm. "For you."

Pa's eyes glistened in the late afternoon sun. "Me? Son—I wanted one of my boys safe. That's why I'm out here."

"But who's going to keep you safe?"

At last, Pa smiled. He bit his lip and then ruffled Tim's hair. "Keep your head down and your rifle loaded. And stick close to me. I won't lose another son."

Tim nodded.

Pa crouched beside him, his gaze tracking toward the barn across the lane.

Tim's regiment held its position above the farm lane for a long time. The rattle of musket fire continued, bullets buzzing past. The lull was over. Federal canisters punctuated the musket drones. Pa still kept watch on that barn. Over the last hour or so, Tim had seen a lot of butternut and gray massing beyond the farm lane. A chill snaked down his spine at the realization. His gut feeling had been right.

"Pa, they're regrouping at the barn," Tim said.

Pa nodded. "Somehow, we've got to scatter the Rebs from it. There's too many to route, but if we can stop them from reforming, then we might be able to hold this line."

The Confeds had already been pushed back from the lane, but what lurked in those haystacks made Tim's skin crawl. He gripped the watch tighter until his fear subsided.

One of Pa's lieutenants shouted for him. Pa snapped up from his position and rushed to meet the thin young man. The lieutenant saluted and Pa returned it as the man spoke quickly. His arms waved and he pointed back toward Mumma's farm. In a crouch, Tim moved down the line toward his Pa until he found Rod McIntyre.

"Something's up, Rod," said Tim and nodded toward the grim-faced lieutenant.

At last, Tim's Pa dismissed the lieutenant. He turned his gaze toward the lane. There was a fearful resignation in his eyes. Captain Adams shouted for attention and the 14th Massachusetts Volunteers turned their unblinking gazes toward him.

"They're going to send us toward that barn," said Tim.

"No," Rod moaned. "It's suicide to send us in there! There's too many Confeds down there just waiting for us to get cocky."

Tim nodded grimly. Rod was right. The entire regiment knew—Pa knew, too. But if the Rebs massed forces there, hard-fought lines at Mumma's swale and Miller's farmhouse might be lost. He gazed at the bodies on the lane below. And all of those soldiers died for nothing.

"Any man able to fire a rifle, fall in!" shouted Captain Adams.

"Help me up," Avery said with a grunt. "I can still shoot!"

Tim and Rod helped Avery to his feet and they stood at attention.

"Fix bayonets!" Captain Adams shouted and attached his bayonet to his rifle.

Tim's stomach clenched as he slid his bayonet into place. With both hands, he held his rifle low on his hip, his never used bayonet glistening in the fading light. How could he use this thing on another man? Gray or blue—how could he gut someone like an animal? He couldn't. He knew if push came to shove, he could not do this.

"Forward, double-time!" ordered his Pa.

As Federal Parrot guns pounded the trees and haystacks, Tim and the 14th Massachusetts Volunteer Rifle regiment advanced toward the farm lane. Tim shielded his eyes as he slipped down from the crest and into the lane. He couldn't look upon their faces and those empty eyes. With cautious steps, he stepped over the dead that lay by the hundreds all down the lane. The lane was eerie with quiet. It seemed to swallow up all the battle sounds. As he slid the pocket watch back into his breast pocket, the gold casing caught the sun's dying rays, giving the watch face an almost shimmery appearance.

Minié balls whispered over their heads from the trees near the farmhouse and out buildings as they hurried onto the hill. Over this hill was another hill that sloped down to those haystacks and concealed God-only-knew how many Confederate soldiers.

Sweat threaded his upper lip and wet his bangs. His breath grew shallow and rapid, the cloying smell of blood receding as he moved toward another cornfield. The pocket watch chain dangled from his pocket with eerie brilliance. The watch against his chest was calming. He could almost feel Chris's presence beside him.

Captain Adams led the regiment into another cornfield. The cornstalks here were tall, not mown down to stumps like most of Mumma's cornfield. He felt safer, more concealed. Besides, twilight was approaching. The fading light and the sulfury smoke would obscure their approach. He hoped the Federal batteries would divert the Rebs' attention.

Several Rebs jumped out from behind small out buildings and haystacks, firing off a barrage of shots that smashed cornstalks but missed men. The regiment returned fire. Tim fired and reloaded quickly. Fired again.

The Rebs abandoned their positions by the haystacks. "Forward!" His Pa ordered. "Toward the barn!"

Tim and Rod zigzagged through the cornfield, Avery staggering beside them. The whole regiment moved closely together, moving more like one entity than thirty-three men. Tim adjusted his pace with Avery's painful movements. The young man had insisted on coming. He was still able to hold and reload his rifle.

As Tim and the others emerged from the cornfield, Captain Adams crested the second hill, the regiment only a few steps behind him. They followed him over the rise.

A line of Rebs emerged from haystacks and trees. The Rebs unleashed a hail of bullets that hissed toward them, felling several men too startled to even cry out.

Men screamed. Line officers fell. The regiment imploded as hot lead slammed into them from all sides. White-hot agony gouged Tim's right side. He cried out, fired, taking out the nearest Reb. He turned, trying to grab Avery, but the young man lay still on the ground.

"Avery!" he shouted, bending toward the young man, but Rod grabbed his arm, pulling him left.

"He's gone! Reload!"

Fighting against the horrible pain in his side, Tim ran. He tore a cartridge then fumbled it into his rifle's muzzle.

"Left flank! Charge!" Captain Adams shouted above the timbre of musket fire and screams.

Rod pulled Tim toward the left flank, following Captain Adams and the remnants of the 14th through the haze. The Rebs pursued them, minié balls shattering the smoky twilight. Ahead, silhouetted against the reddish orange sunset, lay a rail fence. Beyond it, the barn. If they could reach the cover of the barn, they could stand off the Rebs.

Tim and the remains of his regiment struggled over the rail fence.

"To the barn! Charge!" shouted Captain Adams.

The 14th raced across the rough-hewn field toward a white-washed barn.

Rebel shouts and percussion shells thundered around them, the crackle of muskets sharp. The light was starting to fade. Minié balls slashed across their path. Confeds! Rebs rushed toward them from the right flank!

"Keep moving!" Captain Adams screamed. "Don't stop!"

Disoriented in the smoke and dim light, Tim followed Rod blindly through the darkening meadow toward the barn. Doors on both ends were flung wide, the shadowy depths yawning with the unknown. More than half the regiment had been felled in the corn-field. They couldn't hold off several reformed Reb units.

The other soldiers swarmed beside him. Captain Adams and two remaining officers surged into the barn and the light from the far end disappeared. They'd closed the farthest barn door, making sure there was only one way inside.

Tim reached the open barn door at a full tilt run as a volley of Reb shots erupted from the right. He threw himself into the awaiting shadows. Rod and the other soldiers crashed through the threshold beside him.

Captain Adams caught him as he fell and helped him to his feet. Quickly, the captain ordered the regiment into line positions by the only open door.

Twenty feet from the barn door, butternut and gray emerged from the smoke, bayonets fixed. Their faces were bloody and weary, their uniforms powder-burned. Minié balls crackled through the open door, forcing Tim and the others to pull back.

In the distance, percussion shells exploded. Too far away to help them. The fading sunlight was only a bright ember on the horizon. If Tim could somehow signal the batteries, perhaps Federal canister and percussion could cover their escape out the back door?

The pocket watch gleamed in his pocket.

Snatching it free, he held it up into the sunlight. Light caught it, flickering off its surface. He held his side as he angled the light toward the northwest, hoping they'd think it an enemy signal and target the swale.

Lead pounded against the barn as the Rebs advanced, but Tim kept signaling. Finally, Captain Adams jerked him away from the opening as more than two dozen Rebs reached the barn door.

Tim shoved the watch into his pocket and held his rifle with both hands, bayonet pointed toward butternut and gray. Captain Adams and the rest of the regiment stood beside him. He winced. They were severely outnumbered. He'd be joining his brother soon.

The silence in the barn was palpable. Out of the smoky twilight, a Reb rifle muzzle raised toward his Pa.

"No!" Tim screamed. He threw himself in front of Captain Adams as the report echoed through the barn.

Something slammed into his chest and he fell against his pa, knocking them both down.

But no other shots were fired. The Rebs gaped at him, their wide-eyed gazes filled with terror as they stumbled back from the remains of the 14th.

Outside, Federal canister fire thundered against the farmland. Tim smiled. One of the batteries had seen his beacon!

Percussion shells pounded the field near the barn, scattering the Rebs. Not for long, Tim knew. His side burned with fire and he gasped for air.

He felt a hand touch his shoulder and he turned his head, expecting to see his pa's hand, but the ghostly form of his brother knelt beside him. Tim glanced at the remaining soldiers of his unit. Behind them, Chris' entire regiment stood in a shimmery haze. Chris smiled and patted Tim's chest, the touch like a feather, and then he stepped away. He reached out and touched Pa's shoulder before he and his regiment disappeared into the smoke.

"Son, why? Why'd you do a foolish thing like that?" said his Pa, at last finding his voice. His eyes were wet with tears as he tore open Tim's bloodied uniform coat.

"Couldn't let them shoot you," Tim groaned.

Pa laid his hand against Tim's cheek, cupping it. Pa's face was grim. Then his eyes widened as he held up the coat flap. A minié ball had pierced the coat on the left side, but the pocket watch had stopped it from penetrating his chest. The ball was intact, not even flattened against the watchcase. Pa pulled the Minié ball away from the watch face and held it up in the fading light. He tucked the watch into Tim's pants pocket.

Tim sighed. Chris had been at his side the whole time.

Pa laid a handkerchief against the wound in Tim's right side and pressed Tim's hand against it.

After quickly ordering the regiment to fall back to Mumma's swale, Captain Adams and Rod carried Tim out into darkening field. Dodging percussion shells, the regiment slipped out of the field still swarming with Rebs, and back into the cornfield. They hurried across the farm lane and back onto the crest of Mumma's swale. The fighting had eased up with the approaching darkness, but artillery fire still thundered along with occasional musket blasts.

Rod and Captain Adams carried him all the way to Mumma's barn where a makeshift field hospital had been established.

Tim eased the watch from his pants pocket and pressed it to his ear. The second hand ticked steadily. The minié ball hadn't even harmed it. The gleaming watch face read 7:02 p. m., well past sunset. Already, the sky was filling with stars.

The pocket watch still kept perfect time, as it had for four generations.

Night had fallen without the Rebs advancing north or regrouping their forces. With his brother's help, Tim and his regiment held the line against the Rebs. At last, Tim had seen the elephant and survived it.

CENTRAL PREMISE

Leering like a demon, the boy poked at Ruan with a knife. Fear ached deep in the pit of Ruan's stomach and chilled him down to his fingertips. All of his Nurisan senses flared against this obnoxious bully, fighting against his restraint to bubble to the surface and attack. To strike clean and crisp until the threat was gone.

"Come and get it, Ruan," the boy said through clenched teeth.

The boy stepped closer, the brick school house at his back, and Ruan stiffened. He glanced at the teacher standing in the doorway who observed the conflict as she watched clouds drifting slowly past.

The boy flipped a stringy blond lock from his eyes and jabbed the knife at Ruan's chest. "I think his blood has chilled," he said to the crowd of boys and girls surrounding them.

Ruan stared unblinking into the boy's mocking eyes and saw only hatred. To back down would be social suicide . . . but to kill? It was expected that he kill someone who challenged him . . . but this time, something in his conscience struggled against that way. The way of other worlds was different. To die for what they believed in was only acceptable in times of war. They did not understand the commitment behind words like a Nurisan understood.

To the Nurisans, an action and a word were the same, so careful thought went into their words. Still, they retreated from the galaxy, becoming a dark, isolated world to which few travelers dared venture. Of course, when the reigning law was "to the survivor, the spoils belong," who but a Nurisan or a madman would come back here?

The knife zipped past Ruan's face, cutting his left arm. The shock of the pain rippled through him and he stumbled backward, clutching the burning slash. A scream welled deep inside him, an animal cry of battle, and he clenched his fist as the rage made him dizzy. The call of his ancestors wailed in his ears, demanding that he rise up and destroy his attacker, but something held him back.

"Don't push me, Vehrn," he said. From somewhere off to his left a dull beep pulsed for a moment or two then vanished. Somehow the sound was familiar. Wasn't there something he was supposed to do here?

Vehrn snickered. "To study offworld is to study cowardice."

The children's giggles were razors cutting Ruan's soul.

"To study here is to study the ways of animals not people." Those words came out as if memorized, he thought.

Again, the children's white-hot laughter ripped through him. Vehrn slipped behind him and Ruan spun around, not willing to let the boy into his blind spot.

"I hear your words, but I see your walk drags behind them, Ruan-sen."

Another slash. Attaching '-sen' to someone's name labeled them an outsider.

"Look closely," Ruan said. "The mirabi coils low as if to cower, but instead it waits to strike."

The knife blade slashed across Ruan's thigh. He doubled over for a moment, swallowing a cry of pain as Vehrn's high-pitched laughter rang out. Once more, that dull, low-pitched note throbbed and he glanced around, but saw nothing.

"Strike now or cower, mirabi," Vehrn taunted.

Ruan leaped at him, knocking the knife away. They both tumbled to the ground, Ruan pinning Vehrn in the red dirt. Ruan's fists struck out, again and again, until he saw the knife. He swept it up from the ground and held the stained blade to Vehrn's throat, the blood pounding at his temples. Suddenly, he felt the hot breath of the crowd against his neck. Scanning their faces, he saw their fickle switch to his favor at the anticipation of victim and survivor. Sadness sat heavy on his chest. He'd fallen to the call of his ancestors. With a sigh, he turned back to Vehrn. Acceptance flickered in the boy's eyes and mixed with the stubborn, dark pride of Nuris.

"Do I strike now, Vehrn?" he asked and waved the blade under the boy's nose. "or do I walk with the rest of the galaxy?"

"Finish him," someone whispered.

Ruan felt his anger swell again at the pride in Vehrn's eyes that sneered back at him.

"You'll never be one with us again, Ruan-sen. Never."

The movement was fluid as Ruan plunged the knife into Vehrn's chest. The boy cried out and lay still, the burgundy blood bubbling up from the wound. In an instant, a sharp stab gouged Ruan in the neck. He shrieked and clutched his neck, feeling a small device attached there. Again, he heard that low-pitched sound.

"Halt program!"

Instantly, the Nurisan school yard vanished and Ruan found himself kneeling in a detention room. When the humming sound died away, his memory lurched back to him. It was his first school term offworld—away from Nuris.

"What is the Central Premise?" an angry instructor's voice yelled at him from a speaker in the slick gray walls.

Disoriented, he shook his head, trying to remember, but the words did not come. Another sharp pinch in the neck. He cried out this time.

"I don't remember!"

Again, the pain stabbed his neck and he doubled over.

"Didn't you hear the reminder beeps from your OD?"

Ruan groaned and brushed a hand across his neck. The obedience device. "Yes, but my memory was hazy."

"No more violence," the instructor shouted. "You Nurisans and your dark ways. You haven't learned anything yet—and you were their most promising student. How do you expect to be part of humanity when you can't even avoid violence with your own kind? No more violence! Say it."

"No more violence," he muttered.

"Again."

"No more violence."

"You failed the simulation," the instructor barked. "We'll try it again in one week."

"When can I play with the other children?" he asked.

"When we are certain that you won't hurt them."

The door clicked open in front of Ruan. He sighed and rose from the ground. No more violence, he thought. It would be hard to remember that premise with this thing on his neck, but if Nurisans would ever dwell with offworlders, he must forge a path for them. That meant enduring their central premise—at least until they had them outnumbered.

SNOW ANGELS

They adhere to me like rubber gloves, the pliable polymer layers supporting . . . constraining . . . entrapping. At first, I wanted to scream, to twist and shake away the enveloping material and run as hard as I could away—to anywhere—if I still had a physical body. If I had hands, I could feel how my body has been sliced into many iridescent tiers. I realize, after the fear had passed, that all I have is my consciousness and my face . . . with eyes that look out from this holographic representation—a portrait of limbo.

Now, the memories swirl around me, floating past in the layers and one touches me.

"Jerzy, don't!" Lauren giggled and pulled away from me. "Stop tickling me."

The snow was warm beneath us and I no longer felt the numbing wetness seeping into my gloves.

She jumped up from the snow, shaking her brown locks, and frowned. "You've ruined the snow angel."

"I'm sorry."

I pulled myself up from the ground and brushed the wet snow off my coat. After plucking chunks of snow from my sweater, I gazed at the arcs making up the angel's wings. They were pristine, sculpted into the heavy snow. A perfectly symmetrical pair of wings. But the angel's gown was trampled where Lauren had bolted through the snow.

She and I had been making them since we were eight years old. For a long time, we had competed against each other, but as the years passed, we found they were more fun to make together. I pulled her close as I fished a velvety, gray box out of my shirt pocket. "Will this make you forgive me?"

Her brown eyes widened when I opened the box. She cried out, her fingers trembling as she reached for the diamond ring. The square stone glistened like sunlight through icicles.

"Lauren, will you marry me?" Tears rolled down her face as I slipped my high school class ring off her finger and replaced it with the diamond ring. "I can't live my life without you."

"I love you so much," she whispered, her voice cracking.

Her breath was warm against my neck, lips soft and caressing. She was still shaking when I pulled her close.

A sharp pain gouged at the base of my neck. I flinched and pulled away.

"Jerzy, what is it?"

The air sparkled. For an instant, my voice left me. I waited in silence until I could see again.

"Jerzy?"

"I - I'm fine." I said, smiling at her. "Let's go show that ring to your folks."

She returned my smile and led me across the hard-packed snow field.

The memory slides away, caught then strangled, and the polymer presses against me again. I long to reach up and loosen my collar, to move my ghost hands and legs—to stretch. To run and lie with Lauren in the wet snow. I can't even cry . . . the layers are too enclosing. They told me this was the only way and she had agreed. With the tears raining down her face, she had agreed. Said there would still be time for love and snow angels when I was well. She said she'd wait.

For a moment, I can't breathe. I fight to expand my lungs, but realize there's nothing there. They said I would have such sensations for a time, akin to losing limbs, but I would get used to the sensations. Already, I am tired of needing to stretch cramped legs that are not crossed beneath me and I cringe when I'm certain that I smell Lauren's rich Cinnabar. I hate feeling ghost tears well in my eyes and the ache in arms that cannot hold her again. Most of all, I hate not feeling the cold creep into my bones from a Michigan winter.

Before the first Great Dark, all I had was my thoughts. There was no sound, no feeling . . . just the memories and my thoughts. I didn't know it would be like this. I think back to the day they told us and a shiver ripples through me.

Lauren's face turned snow white and she collapsed back in the chair. She couldn't look the doctor or me in the eye and I was relieved. I didn't want her to see the tears welling in my eyes. I didn't want her to see my fear.

"Can't you do anything?" she pleaded. "Chemo? Radiation? Macrobiotics?" Her hand wrapped around mine, clutching so hard that my fingers ached. "Anything?"

The doctor shook her head. "I'm sorry. The cancer has reached stage three. And the tumor is inoperable."

She covered her face and I pulled her against me. Her Cinnabar comforted me. For the moment, she was still there. I was still there.

Her face dissolves into the translucent layers that hang all around me. The delicate curves of her oval face slip through my ghost fingers and I long for her cedary smell and the touch of her delicate fingers wrapped around mine.

Even her anger makes me smile now. I made her a snow angel that day. I didn't feel like it and when she saw my legs and arms swishing in the snow, she started to cry again. I pulled myself up from the snow and put my arms around her, trampling the angel's left wing as I reached out.

"Why do you always do that," she shouted.

"Do what?"

"Ruin our snow angel? It was perfect and now you've ruined it!" She turned away, her voice raw with agony. I could do nothing to comfort her.

They told me that cryogenics was a waste of time, that in the future, the cryo tubes would be misunderstood and shut off. Holographic stasis was best, they said. It would store my genetic code, my consciousness and a holographic representation of my body. From this map, they could bring me back—and cure my cancer.

Now, as I stare out of the rainbowed polymer layers, I know I've been cheated out of the last days of my life with Lauren.

During the first Great Dark, I learned how to connect the holographic layers of sight then smell then touch. I thought that I might see her again, but that never happened. For a long while, I saw only whiteness. White floors, white gowns and white tile. Then the Dark returned.

I know now that so much time has passed and that terrifies me. How much time? Where had this holographic stasis placed me? I somehow feel that I'm not in the lab anymore and that makes me shake.

Every once in a while, sounds pierce the silence. A word or disjointed phrase.

"No," says a disembodied voice, the tinny sound reverberating through the layers. "No, I don't think so. His nose is too wide. What about this one?"

A blinding flash of light shocks me. I swear that tears are rolling down my face. Light! The second Great Dark has ended—and I can hear now. I can hear! Another layer connected.

Strange hazel eyes framed by bushy eyebrows stare back at me. Horrified, I attempt to pull away, but the polymer is too rigid. I long to cover my eyes. I feel my arms at my side, their weight, the dull ache in invisible shoulders, but all I can do is gaze off to the side.

The head shakes. "No. Don't care for this vintage one either. He looks ill. Do you have any clown faces?"

When the head glides past, I see a sign that hangs in a window, 'The Mind's Eye: a holographic gallery of art.' A chill rolls across my face and my teeth chatter. What have they done to me? Suddenly, everything tilts.

"Here, let me straighten that frame for you," rumbles another voice.

My view snaps back to center again. What have they done to me? There are other holographic images framed on the wall across from me. Dear God. I'm just another print for sale!

I want to cry out to Lauren, but I know she is long gone from this world.

"I've heard that in the past, they used some sort of genetic digitizing to preserve terminally ill patients."

A laugh, like fingers on a chalkboard, reverberates through the layers. "That's just another urban legend."

What happened to Lauren? How many other people like me hang in this gallery? Oh God. Time has spiraled away from me. Horror cuts cold and deep into my stomach.

They've lost the technology to make me live again—or even to let me die now. Either way, I have lost Lauren. I feel like a snow angel etched in plastic, waiting to melt in the Spring thaw. I hope Spring comes early. What good is a snow angel with one wing?

RENA 733

There wasn't much left of #733. Hardly enough to bury, much less autopsy. Another dead soldier from the multitude of colonization squadrons. I snapped on my rubber gloves, hating this job, and peeled back the body bag flaps.

I never called the soldiers by anything other than their tag number, but this one was so young—no more than twenty. Seeing another half-faced, burned body made me ill. I couldn't help myself, the name Rena just popped into my head. Her one eye, green, stared strangely content past me as I sloshed her remains onto the chrome table. Stale blood scent mixed with germicide. I scanned the reclamation orders on the side of the bag with a light pen: recover one microfeed and one MRC. A memory replacement chip. My hands began to shake.

I shifted Rena 733's body toward the small image capture scanner at the edge of the table. The red light winked on and encircled her head, gathering streams of data from the MRC.

The scanner hummed, converting the raw data into an enhanced viewable format. EVF produced a third person video effect of the stored memories. The data could only be converted to EVF once. In a few moments, a summary scan of the chip, only the last 48 hours of this soldier's life, would be played back on the screen above my head. Sometimes, MRCs were damaged by the extraction, so this prescan was a failsafe. The HQ suits had to have their data.

The autopsy room door slid open and medtech student, Deanna Fitzsimmons entered the chamber. Her bobbed blonde hair lay flat against her pale cheeks and thin face. This was Deanna's first week at the station and already, she reminded me a lot of myself back in medical school. It had been more than a year since I last worked with a partner. Deanna's face contorted when she glanced at the body on the table.

"Another one?" She inhaled sharply. "That's the fifteenth casualty since lunch. Don't you get tired of this, Doctor?"

I leaned against the table, studying Deanna's tired blue eyes and the fine lines beginning around her nose and mouth. She wasn't much older than Rena 733. I hated throwing so many cases at her in her first week, but she'd have to get used to dealing with the bodies.

"I don't think I can look at another one today," I said, surprised by the weariness in my voice. I knew Deanna couldn't handle another autopsy like this one today. "Why don't you take log duty this time?"

Deanna smiled, relieved by my suggestion. She turned away from the table and picked up the datapad that hung on the far wall. She scrolled through the chart and her gaze snapped up, looking past Rena 733—even past me. "Ready whenever you are, Dr. Kingston."

"Good," I said. "We'll begin as soon as the data capture is complete."

"When do you match tags with names?"

"I don't. They handle that back on Earth," I answered. And for that, I was thankful.

I glanced up, seeing the blank screen, then flicked on the autopsy laser. Deanna flinched at the sound. The chrome fixtures cast the scanner's red sheen against the shiny gray, tiled walls and floor. Deanna walked over to the space station portal as I cut open Rena 733's cranium.

Voices echoed through the chamber and I looked up to see desert stretching into velvet, umber hills on the viewscreen, the horizon a mixture of creams and rust. The barrel of Rena 733's Stupor plasma rifle, slung over one shoulder, bobbed at the edge of the viewscreen.

Twenty. I cringed, gazing from Rena 733's burned face to

Deanna's pale profile. I remembered being twenty once. Before medical school. Before the Antaris War. Before computer retro-viruses crippled the nets and we lost most of our private technology to the government. I sighed. Before MRCs. Hundreds of soldiers had come through this station, but until today, it had never both-ered me. Only another report to upload. Still, I wondered if it was Deanna or the MRC that disturbed me most.

I reached up to shut off the output. I didn't want to know anymore than I had to—it just made my job harder.

"What are you doing?" Deanna asked.

"Shutting off the MRC's output."

Deanna frowned. "Don't you want to know who she was?"

I shook my head and looked away from the screen.

"But why? She's out there protecting our world. She should be given more respect than a number."

I set down the laser. "Do you really understand what an MRC is?" I asked, knowing at best, she'd only read about them.

"It records—"

I shook my head. "No, Deanna, it *parses*. It selectively parses out memories and feeds back only the ones that pass the algorithm. Anything that causes adverse emotional reactions to the job is quickly and permanently parsed out."

Deanna's face whitened. "God. How horrible."

"The parsed out memories remain on the chip, so HQ can access them. But she can't. I don't want to invade her privacy."

Reaching up to the screen, I laid my hand against the shut off switch, but something made me stop. "Are you sure you want to see this? I don't."

She had that passerby look on her face, that mixture of revulsion and unblinking curiosity that people displayed at the scene of a tragedy. Finally, she nodded. "In case she had a last request or some-thing," she said in a small voice.

I pulled my hand away, dreading the playback. Only once had I allowed myself to watch one of these before.

On the screen, another soldier crouched beside Rena 733, his sandy hair tousled and his face sweaty. He examined claw-like footprints, dipping a gloved hand into the fine, gold sand. "No sign of them, Gates," said the man. "Continue tracking or return to camp?"

"Are we seeing through her eyes?" Deanna asked.

"Sort of. The many layers of images and points of view are brought together so we see this soldier as well as what she saw and felt."

"Her name's Gates," said Deanna.

I sighed. Yes, she was right. Rena 733 had a real name, but in her present state, I found that fact too painful.

"They can't be far, Ryan," Gates answered in a smooth, alto voice. "The Colonel wants a position report before 19:00."

"Until we find our patrol's insides strung out like streamers, those Antaran bastards won't show themselves."

"Shut up, Ryan," Gates said and squinted at the horizon. Her thoughts whispered through the speakers, the tone softer and echoing due to the computer enhancement of her thoughts.

I tried not to watch the screen, but I couldn't help myself.

What if we do find them? What then? I'm not afraid and I should be. Why do I want so desperately to go after the Antarans like this? I even dream about it. I want to come out here and fight . . . except when I'm here. What's the matter with me? Gates rubbed her face and gripped the rifle tighter.

"She doesn't know," I said in a half-whisper, my mouth falling open. "My God, they put those things in her head and didn't even tell her."

Ryan stood up, brushing the sand off his beige uniform. "Gates? Do you ever—No, forget it," he said, waving her off.

She frowned and turned toward him. "What? Do I ever what?"

He gazed down at the ground, parting the sand into a semi-circle with the toe of his boot. "Do you ever . . . well, fear these encounters?"

"Sometimes. Do you?"

He nodded. "I feel like pissing my pants right now."

Why aren't I that scared? She pointed toward a bluff in the distance. "We'll hike out to there and go back to base if we turn up nothing."

"Agreed," said Ryan, who shoved his rifle back over his shoulder.

Gates moved in front of him, her boots whisking across the sand, but Ryan's scream forced her to turn—too late. Talons blurred. A spiky appendage burst up from the sand, piercing Ryan's body. He screamed again. Sliding the plasma rifle into her hands, Gates squeezed off a volley of blasts into the sand until something screeched. The appendage splattered into an inky puddle beside Ryan's crumpled body.

She collapsed beside him and pulled him up from the ground, one arm balancing the plasma rifle that quivered at the edge of the viewscreen. He wheezed, blood dripping from his nose and mouth, intestines dangling from his torso. He grabbed her sleeve.

Oh, God. Don't die on me! Please don't die! "Hang on, Ryan—I got you!"

"Gates, I—Gates—" His hand fell away from her sleeve.

"Sssh, don't talk now." *Why Ryan? Why! We went through boot camp together.* Her hushed voice reverberated again.

Oh, God, he's dying.

I turned away when Gates began to sob, the rawness in her voice grating.

"My God," said Deanna. "Her best friend just got killed!" She let the datapad fall onto a counter top and she looked away from the screen.

"They're both at peace now," I offered.

"At peace? He was ripped apart and she was blown to pieces!"

I studied Deanna's reddening face, the tears rimming her eyes. "Death is a part of life and we have to accept that. You have to accept that if you're going to be a Frontline Tech."

The anger twisting her features surprised me. She didn't even know these people.

"And you need to understand that when you open those bags, there are people inside—not numbers."

"That's why this job never gets easier," I said, turning toward Rena 733, and picked up the tissue-resin separator from the instrument tray.

My stomach ached when I sifted through the remains of Rena 733's cerebrum and midbrain for the microfeed. The nanoprocessor controlled microfeed was activated by combat and controlled aggression and its effects—adrenalin rushes, endorphin releases. I shook my head. Poor kid was addicted to battle. Kept her out there fighting just to feel good. Craving the kill like some psychopath. This was the third soldier I had seen beta-testing these new combat enhancements.

"Make a note on the chart that Rena 733 is another combat technology beta-tester, Fitzsimmons."

"All this technology and yet this war goes on forever," said Deanna, not diverting her gaze from the viewscreen. She didn't even look at the datapad as she typed.

She was right. Too many people were dying and with every territory we gained, we lost one somewhere else. It was a stalemate at best. When I was a first year, I had Deanna's idealism. I remember standing at the armed forces' recruitment desk, fresh out of med school on a mission of mercy. I wanted to go to the front and save lives. Back then, like Gates, I didn't know the cost. Didn't even understand it. Not sure I did now.

Busying myself with the extractions, I shut out the viewscreen's sounds of shifting sand as Gates carried Ryan back to camp. I found the ATP-driven microfeed lodged in Rena's brain stem. It had been surgically implanted high into her brain's third ventricle, but whatever explosive she had stepped on must have caused the microfeed to dislodge and pierce the brain stem.

As I probed deeper, I found that some bastard surgeon had removed her amygdalae so she couldn't develop a fear of the enemy. Even the hippocampus had been altered, an MRC attached to it. I shuddered at the sight of the tiny, black chip containing all her memories. It hijacked her ability to form new ones, storing all of them into the chip and then selectively parsing out everything but the harmless memories for transmission. Working with the tissue-resin separator, I carefully dislodged the microfeed.

I watched as Gates entered her base camp and then her barracks. Abruptly, the screen went dark, the computer parsing out sleep and dream sequences. I sighed. Gates only had twenty-four hours left. Twenty years old with twenty-four hours to live.

The screen suddenly blurred to daylight, Gates fumbling out of her barracks in full field gear. One of the other soldiers approached.

"Sorry to hear about Ryan, Heather," said the soldier, shaking her head. "Tough break. I know how close you two were."

"What are you talking about?" Gates asked.

"I heard about the ambush yesterday. I'm really sorry."

What's she talking about? I didn't hear about any ambush. There was a Ryan in boot camp, but not out here. She's been offworld too long. "Right—thanks," Gates mumbled. "When do we frag the Antaris camp?"

I gripped the edge of the table. That bastard chip had even parsed out Ryan's existence. It didn't even leave her a memory of her best friend.

The other soldier checked her watch. "T minus six hours. We have to wait for an orbit window. Can't go in with those satellites firing at us and our shuttle cover."

I extracted the memory replacement chip and mumbled through my own personal damage assessment, accounting for lost limbs, obliterated organs, and cause of death. Too bad "blown to bits" wasn't anywhere on my medical ROMs. Her legs and half her chest were gone. The only real thing left of Rena 733, the only thing that contained anything that was once her, was the memory replacement chip. It contained Rena 733's entire career as a soldier—and her last days. To the government, it was only beta test data and now the suits would see it all, whether she had wanted them to or not.

"Open computer log. Autopsy #733, Dr. Jeannette Kingston presiding, Deanna Fitzsimmons assisting."

For the computer log, I rolled off a string of observations, "Enhancement of reticular formation still intact, limbic system remained functional at time of death . . . " For the government report that would be coredumped into some net info tomb.

"So, when you going home, Gates," asked a voice from the viewscreen. I turned around again, seeing Gates marching beside a weather-beaten soldier with haggard gray eyes.

"End of the month they tell me. Guess my tour's up. I'll miss it." *And that scares me. I miss Mom and Dad. Haven't even seen my new niece yet, but leaving the troop scares the hell out of me. Makes me feel sick. What will I do?*

My eyes misted. That new niece was probably in school now, but she didn't know that. More memories stolen, parsed away by the MRC. It was all stored in the chip, but she couldn't access it. My hands began to shake again. They didn't even let her remember her best friend beyond boot camp. Couldn't let a soldier form attachments. When one died, that memory was parsed into the bit bucket. Soldiers couldn't care about anything out here. Neither could doctors. What had they done to this girl? Gates was hard around the edges, addicted to combat and unafraid of an enemy that had shredded her to ribbons. The suits had made her into some animal with its instinct removed. How many soldiers had they done this to? But this soldier was different now; she had a name, emotions—a family.

I set down the tissue-resin separator, the distant memory of a little girl brought into emergency once when I was in residency. She had drowned in a swimming pool when her father had left her alone in the backyard. They had revived her en route, but she died before I could even tube her. Where had that memory come from? I hadn't thought about that in years. My eyes filled with tears. In medical school, one of my professors had warned me that there'd be a handful of cases that would stay with me. I guess this was one of those cases.

Biting my lip, I tried not to look at Rena 733's face, but I couldn't stop myself. In the remains of her face, I saw that child's desperate, pleading green eyes suddenly turn dull, the monitor flat-lining with a screech. I had just stood there, the endotracheal tube dangling from my hand. Dammit, it wasn't supposed to be this way here. That's why they all had numbers and no names. It was too hard when they had names—and pasts. I looked away from Rena 733's half-face and with shaking hands, I picked up the tissue-resin separator again. Why couldn't I stop shaking?

Suddenly, I felt Rena 733's blood on my gloves. Hopes and

dreams ran through it. Anger and tears. Twenty years' worth. Like Deanna. Rena 733 was more than bone to cut through or blood needed for typing and DNA extraction. She was more than autopsy #733.

Carefully, I laid the memory replacement chip in a tray beside the microfeed. Moving to the processing equipment to the right of the table, I sent the chip through. The instrument whirred and groaned, converting all the information into its final enhanced viewable format. All the suits required now was a viewer and they could access all Gates' memories.

On the viewscreen, Heather Gates screamed as the ground exploded beneath her, throwing her several meters across the sand. For an instant, she survived the blast. Her gaze traveled up to the sky. "Mom, I need you," she gurgled, but in a moment, the viewscreen winked out and the processing unit stopped. The summary scan had concluded. Heather Gates' life was over.

"They'll see it all, won't they?" Deanna asked in a small voice. "And she won't even know about it. It isn't fair."

I picked up the chip from the tray. Gates' entire soldiering career lay on this chip, private moments, personal feelings belonging only to Heather Gates. And so much of it had been cut off from her memory. Cheated away from her by this MRC.

"You're right, Deanna," I said. "It isn't fair."

I dropped the little memory prison onto the table. Part of Gates' life had been in my hands, like that little girl's had been and all those soldiers on the front line. Case numbers blurred with blood types and bar codes as I picked up a wide-handled clamp. Those soldiers had lives before they came to me. Heather Gates did too and so did I once.

"Computer, pause autopsy record #733."

Slamming the clamp handle against the MRC, I pounded it and pounded it until it was shards of resin and silicon. The crunching of silicon filled the silence and I cherished the sound. It wasn't bone splitting or a body bag unzipping. It was my anger and there was nothing the government could do about it. Deanna stood frozen beside the table, her mouth gaping.

"If Heather Gates wasn't allowed to remember these things, then the government won't get the privilege either."

"Computer, resume autopsy record #733. Note: MRC did not survive the blast. Only shards detected throughout the cortex and cerebrum. Fragments will follow under separate cover. End record. End report." I motioned toward Deanna.

"Send the report, please."

While Deanna uploaded the report, I gathered the MRC fragments into a small container. Heather Gates' memories would stay her own—for how ever long she had them. It was the only shred of dignity I could offer her now.

I barcoded the cause of death information into a label that I printed and attached to the body bag. I didn't need to see a viewscreen to know how she died. After microsuturing the remains of Gates back together, I laid her to rest in the body bag.

I zipped up the body bag and then laid a hand against my neck, knowing that tomorrow I wouldn't remember Heather Gates or my conversation with Deanna. Heather Gates would be #733 again.

"Doctor Kingston," said Deanna, her voice soft. "I've been wanting to ask—why did you call her Rena?"

"Computer, scan KingstonJL."

I closed my eyes as the white scan light slid across me.

"Why are you doing that?" Deanna asked.

"Display report on screen." I pointed to the computer viewscreen. "Read it, Deanna."

"Why?" she asked, shaking her head.

"Just read it."

Her gaze flitted across the data and I read it with her. Every day, it was new to me, too. Finally, she gasped and her gaze jerked toward me. Tears welled in my eyes.

"You've got an MRC."

I nodded. "This job required it. I used to write myself notes when I got out of the hospital, so I wouldn't forget anything. Now, I just append them into my login scripts."

"Why didn't you turn down the job?" Her eyes were wide.

"Turn it down?" I laughed bitterly. "I volunteered for it!"

"You volunteered?"

"I thought it would be better than dying inside every time a soldier died." Or a child. I leaned against the table. "Better than crying my heart out for months and months after a child died in my arms. I thought working with numbers would be easier. That way I wouldn't die inside. I didn't know the MRC was just another way to die." And I didn't know the government would take away memories they had no right to take.

The silence was palpable and I wanted to reach out and shove it aside. Deanna could only stare at me, a tear funneling down her cheek.

"I'm so sorry," she finally whispered.

"Every morning, when I log into the system, I play back a history file that I create every night. But it isn't enough. Words on a screen meant for someone else. I'm living in the third person, Deanna."

I laid my hand on the body bag, wanting to exchange places with Heather Gates.

Deanna walked over to me and squeezed my arm. "It's all right, Doctor. You don't have to answer my question."

I felt the sobs ache through me, my knees trembling with weakness. "But I do. Rena was the name of my daughter, Rena Diane Kingston. She would have been twenty-one this month." I sucked in a deep breath. "She drowned when she was two. When I finished my residency, the government thought it best to parse out her memory—without my consent. When I took this job, I didn't know they would take away my daughter's memory."

"How . . . did you find out?"

I picked up a shard of the MRC left behind on the examination table. "Their algorithm cleaned my memories of Rena, but their chip couldn't totally parse my child from my thoughts. It only pushed her back until she became a nameless child in ER. It was the best the bastards could do. But they missed one thing."

Deanna stared at me for a moment. "What was that?" she said finally in a soft voice.

"My ex-husband. I lost track of him when he joined the Service until—" I sighed. "Until he came through here. And it was all there in his MRC, my daughter, the accident, the divorce—everything."

Deanna shook her head. "But your memory would have been—"

"Parsed out? Most of it, maybe, but not out of my login script. What happened to her and who she was will always be there—every time I log in."

Pressing against the MRC shard, I snapped it between my fingers and let the pieces fall to the floor. I would remember and mourn my daughter whether they let me or not. Rena Diane Kingston. She had a name again and I would remember it.

THE MERMAID'S
LOOKING GLASS

Waves scoured the beach in a restless froth and roar of water, carving the sand into rough trenches. A steady wind stroked Lily Pratt's short hair as she stood on the 33rd Street turnaround, rain misting her face. Nelscott, Oregon had been a different place in 1920, not the conglomerate of towns it was today. Regardless of city boundaries, the beach had changed little. The ocean's power was raw and wild, still able to tear families apart.

Below the turnaround, a mother, grandparents, and a two-year-old, all wrapped in windbreakers, scurried across the beach. The adults turned their back on the ocean and Lily's heart pounded into her throat, watching the child scamper toward the water. The ocean roiled and water surged closer. The child tottered, his path unchanged.

At last, the mother turned and hurried toward the child. Lily's muscles went slack, relieved the child hadn't been swept out to sea.

She'd seen rogue waves strike without warning on these beaches, tossing massive logs like splinters and towing them out to sea. Light-headed, she sank down on a nearby bench, remembering a long ago child on this beach. Not even eighty years could erase that haunting trail of little footprints leading across the sand toward the ocean.

"Grandma, are you all right?" Lily's granddaughter, Samantha rushed from her white Nissan to the stone benches. Divorced, in her early thirties, Samantha was getting her life on track again. Lily appreciated her granddaughter and was grateful for their close relationship. Samantha had the Pratt's dark good looks.

"I'm not made of glass," Lily replied.

Her body felt tired, but not ninety-seven years old. She had never gotten used to the contradiction of aging. With every year piled onto her body, her mind let it go. Instead, her mind whirled around the accumulation of things unresolved, acts unexplained, and guilt unshaken.

All of that had brought her here, with the help of her granddaughter. There would be an end to it.

Samantha sat down beside her on the bench and slid an arm around her waist. "I know, but I still worry," she answered. "And I get that honestly."

Lily put her arm around Samantha, gazing at the houses perched on the hills above the ocean. Back in 1920, all of this had been hillside and somewhere near 33rd street stood the Pratt summer home. The Victorian house had overlooked the beach, its sandy trails winding down the hillside. (The house burned to the ground in 1958, long after Lily's father had sold it.)

"I didn't think I'd recognize anything," said Lily, her gaze tracing memories across the rows of houses and concrete retaining walls. "But it feels familiar." Tasting the salt on her lips, Lily could almost feel the shifting sands beneath her feet.

"Okay, now what's the big secret?" Samantha asked, rising from the bench. "What was it that you would never tell us?"

It sounded so grand, so mysterious—a family secret. She wished it had been something wondrous and innocent, something satisfying to at last tell. But Lily had held the secret out of respect for her three sisters. Now that Ruth had been gone two months now, it was time to let it all go.

Lily set her purse in her lap and opened the beige vinyl bag. Cupping her hand, she slid out a blue and green swirled glass float. Inside its warm surface, a milky substance blossomed then dissipated in a continuous slow stream.

"What is that?" Samantha asked, peering closer.

"One night in June of 1920, it washed up on the Nelscott public beaches. I found it while beachcombing."

Samantha reached out a hand toward it, but Lily pulled it back.

"Don't touch it," she said in a sharp voice, putting her hand between the float and Samantha's fingers.

"Why?" Samantha asked, eyes wide. She frowned. "Is it fragile?"

Over the years, Lily had tried to crush it, bury it, and sell it, but it always returned unharmed to Ruth—like a bad penny. When it turned up in Ruth's things, Lily realized it had to be returned to this place.

"You're far more fragile than this hunk of—" Of what? Other than its curse, she knew no more about this sphere than she had in 1920. "Listen to me. In 1920, a child died on this beach, killed by a rogue wave."

Samantha pointed at the float. "And it had something to do with that thing?"

Lily nodded and put the awful sphere back into her purse. "Let's talk about it tonight at the hotel." She stood up and moved toward the concrete steps. Gazing out at the pounding surf, she gathered her memories and the landscape around her.

Lily remembered the long car trips from Portland to Nelscott, the elaborate preparations her mother had made. Lily had been one of four daughters, so any trip was a major undertaking in those days. At fourteen, Lily was still more interested in tomboy things than suitors and marriage, suffering the bows and ribbons adorning her dresses as long as she had marbles in her pockets.

Her sister, delicate, doe-eyed Sophie was two years older and seeing one boy, Mark Tilton, exclusively. Distraught and melodramatic over her forced separation from Mark for eight weeks, Sophie moped about in her finest dresses like Theta Barrow. Of course, Sophie tried to turn the back seat of Daddy's new Ford's into a fainting couch, but a quick shot of marbles into her cheek cleared up that problem.

"Lily, stop it!" Sophie shrieked and shot up in her seat, holding a red spot on her cheek.

"I will when you stay on your side of the car."

"Both of you act your age and stop it," Daddy said with a growl, glancing at us. Neither girl needed to be told again.

Sighing loudly, Sophie draped herself against the back window. "Oh, I wish Mark were here."

"Me, too," said Lily, gathering up her brightly colored clay marbles from the vibrating seat. "It would be much quieter back here."

"Mom, when are Ruth and Phillip arriving?" Sophie asked, ignoring Lily.

Ruth was Lily's oldest sister. Married three years with a toddler named Thad. He was the first Pratt grandchild. Daddy and Mom were so proud of that tow-headed little boy.

"They're already at the house with Clara."

Nobody talked about how Clara, Lily's youngest sister, was different. Clara rarely spoke and always seemed to be in her own little world except for moments when Daddy read to them after supper. Dark hair and eyes like Sophie, there was a plainness about Clara, as if all her energy was focused inward. Mother said it wasn't her fault. She'd just been born inside herself.

Lily liked to imagine Clara was a princess trapped in fairyland, like the woman called Opal in the stories Daddy read from his Atlantic Monthly. Opal Whiteley wrote about fairies and little winged creatures in her diary and Lily liked those stories best.

At last, the five-hour car ride ended with the winding jaunt down Anchor Street. The house stood tall on the windy hills, its cedar shingles gray and weather worn. Lily loved the little attic bedroom that looked out over the Pacific. It was small and smelled of moth balls, but Lily loved its sloped ceiling and little nooks.

Ruth rushed out the front door in her periwinkle dress, white apron tied around her tiny waist.

"Mother!" she cried and embraced her.

Phillip followed her out, Thad in his arms, and everyone hugged and chattered. Except for Clara. Lily knew she'd find her little sister by the window somewhere. As if waiting for some prince to rescue her from her silent tower.

Lily ran her fingers through the heather that tumbled over the rocks in front of the house. A hedge of wild roses bloomed red and pink along the side of the house. In the grayness, bright green moss softened the hard edges of the world as she stepped back and watched Thad's hurried but awkward steps to Mother who scooped him up and showered him with kisses. He giggled, snuggling against her while Sophie talked Ruth's ear off about Mark. Phillip and Daddy walked behind, hands in their pockets, talking about the car. It was good to be in Nelscott.

Wandering across the wraparound porch, Lily stepped inside, through the living room and into the back parlor where nine-year-old Clara sat by the window.

"Hi, Clara," she said, sitting down in the blue spoon-backed chair.

Clara didn't turn toward her. She kept her gaze on the ocean, hands folded in her lap.

"We had a nice ride down from Portland," Lily began and talked about Sophie's boyfriend, the neighbor's tabby that had kittens, and anything else Clara might have missed. Clara never seemed like she heard Lily, but Lily wanted to include her all the same. She waved goodbye to Clara and clattered outside toward the hill path leading to the ocean.

"Lily, you be careful down there," her mother called out the window. "Don't turn your back on that ocean."

Lily rolled her eyes and skittered down the path to comb the beach for treasures.

That evening, Samantha and Lily checked into the Sand Castle Motel. It was a modest blue and gray building that faced the ocean. Lily had trouble with the stairs, but she took each one slowly until she reached the second floor. Samantha carried both bags upstairs to a blue room with two double beds. Exhausted, Lily sat down on the bed, the room smelling stuffy.

"Samantha, open a window, please."

She slid open the window, letting in the roar of the sea. Lily loved that sound.

Samantha plopped into a chair by the window. "It must have been something to have the Pacific as your backyard."

"I used to love the summers down here," Lily answered, the aches deep in her bones. She closed her eyes, feeling the weight of the strange float in her purse.

Samantha's gaze fell to the purse. "Until that thing came?"

Lily nodded.

"Tell me about it." Samantha sighed. "Grandma, I really want to understand why you came all this way for a float."

She took the float out of her purse, its milky interior undulating like waves, and threw it against the wall. Samantha cringed as the float smacked the wall then thudded against the carpet.

"To get rid of that thing forever. I never want to see it again! It doesn't break, it doesn't change, but it has an insidious way of breaking everything around it."

Samantha rose and started toward the float.

"Leave it!"

"But Grandma—"

"Leave it! It goes back to the ocean tomorrow. Now, sit down and listen."

Lily hadn't wanted to be so cross, but Samantha didn't understand yet. She needed to understand.

"All right, tell me about the float," said Samantha, sitting down in her chair again.

The best time to look for treasures was at high tide. Little wooden boxes with Japanese writing, glass fishing floats, those were some of Lily's favorites. But on this day, the little blue and green globe embedded in the sand was something Lily had never seen before. When she held the swirled colors up to the cloudy sky, it made the clouds change from blues to greens. She'd never found a glass float like it before.

She rushed up the sandy path and onto the back porch. "Mother, look what I found! Look what I found!"

Mother hurried into the room, Thad scuttling after her.

Lily held up the float.

"Lily, it's beautiful," she said. "You'll have to hang it from the porch with your others."

Grinning, Lily carried it through the house like a trophy, sand clinging to her pale yellow dress, and tried to find Phillip or Sophie. She walked into the parlor where Clara sat by the window.

"Clara, look!" said Lily and held out the float to her.

Her gaze flicked from the window and she stared.

"See what I found in the ocean? Isn't it pretty?"

Lily reached out to Clara's hands and put the float into her palm. Clara's lips pursed as she stared into the float. Then the moment of connection was gone as she floated off into her own little world again.

"You can keep it," she told Clara and left her with the float.

That evening at supper, amid the smell of yeast rolls and rosemary, Father said blessings and served the pot roast. Moments later, Clara appeared in the doorway, the float in her hands. She walked into the room, down the long table and around to the window where she sat down and stared out the window. Mother watched her, a little surprised, then continued to eat.

For two more nights, Clara entered the room at supper time and sat in the same room while the family ate. But the third night she appeared in the doorway, she walked to the end of the long table and stopped. Taking hold of a cane back chair, she pulled it out and sat down beside Ruth.

"Clara, are you going to eat with us?" Lily asked. She couldn't remember a meal with Clara at the table. For as long as she could remember, Clara's disconnection had been total.

Clara nodded at her.

Mother dropped her fork and the room fell silent. Tears welled in Mother's eyes and Lily realized how much that small interaction had meant.

Over the next week or two, the changes in Clara were dramatic. Every evening after supper, Daddy read to the family. Sophie sat on the sofa, leaning against Phillip. Ruth laid her head on Phillip's shoulder. Mother sat on the other sofa beside Daddy. Clara walked in and smiled.

"Good evening," she said in a sweet voice and sat on the floor at Mother's feet.

Mother was overcome. She wrapped her arms around Clara and cried. Clara hadn't spoken a word since she was four. Daddy stopped reading. Always Clara carried the float and Lily began to notice that the clear float had grown opaque, the glass almost milky.

Thad tottered over to Clara. Grinning, he pointed at the float.

"Ball," he said.

Clara nodded at him.

Again, he pointed and said, "Ball."

"That's right, Thad," said Ruth, leaning forward. "Ball."

Thad bent down and pointed a third time. Then he looked at Clara again. "Have ball."

Clara's eyes darkened. "No," she snapped.

"Have ball," said Thad again, insistent.

"No," she said and pulled the float away.

Thad began to cry. Ruth quickly scooped him up and distracted him with another toy. No one said a word to Clara, but Lily noticed how she clung to the glass sphere.

Samantha rose from her chair and lay down on the opposite bed. She propped her chin up on her elbows and turned on the light by the bed. "So, you think that float had some sort of power?"

"At first," she answered. "But later—" She sighed. "There's a power in that thing, but I misunderstood it. And I didn't know what it was capable of."

"But it obviously helped your sister, didn't it?"

Lily's eyes stung and she bit her lip. "For a while. Then things got weird."

For the first time in her life, Lily had a conversation with Clara. She and Clara talked about Sophie's temper, Mother's sugar cookies, and how Clara liked to watch Lily's marbles bounce across the oak floor boards.

"I used to imagine that you were a princess trapped in a fairyland," said Lily to her sister.

Clara smiled, stroking the sphere. "I was afraid you just thought I was dumb."

Lily shook her head. "I'm glad you've come home again. Sophie doesn't like to do anything but girl things."

Clara cocked her head. "Girl things?"

"You know," said Lily, turning a glass marble over and over in her palm, "doing her hair, picking out clothes in the Roebuck catalog, that kind of stuff." She made a sour face. "Sophie doesn't want to get sand on her button ups, so she won't even go down to the beach."

A wistful look touched Clara's bright face. She looked more and more like Sophie every day, no longer plain but vibrant.

"I've never been to the beach," she said, her gaze on the milky sphere again.

"Never?" Lily cried.

Clara shook her head.

"Come on," said Lily with a grin and grabbed Clara's arm.

They raced through the parlor, out the back door, and down the sandy path to the beach. Clara froze, obviously stunned.

"It's so loud," she shouted above the waves.

"Mother says never to turn your back. Sometimes big waves hit and you can get pulled off the beach."

"Into the water," said Clara with a wistful sigh. She hugged the float to her stomach, but a faint smile remained. She edged forward a few steps at a time. Lily ran ahead then stopped, waiting for Clara to catch up until they were at the frothy edge of the water. Rainbow bubbles danced across the dark sand and Lily kicked through them.

She and Clara giggled.

"Sometimes when I'm really mad," said Lily, "I come out here and scream as loud as I can into the waves." Lily leaned out, the salty water splashing her face, and screamed as a nearby wave crashed against the beach.

"Try it," she said to Clara.

As the next wave rolled in, she and Clara screamed long and hard until Lily's throat hurt. Then they ran from the next wave rushing toward their feet. Clara's laughter rose above the rush of water as she threw out her arms in the surge of water. It was the most musical sound Lily had ever heard. She danced with the gulls that flitted across the wet sand, the water white and foamy across her bare feet.

From the edge of the water, Lily watched her play, her eyes full of tears. At last, Clara was free from her prison.

Hours later, they returned to the porch. Lily felt exhausted, but Clara seemed barely winded, a smile on her face as she sat on the porch steps. Clara gazed down at the path to the beach then at the house. Her smile fell as she reached out and squeezed Lily's arm.

"I can't stay in there anymore," Clara said in a soft, aching voice that nearly took Lily's breath. "Not forever."

"I'll help you."

"Thank you," she whispered. At the sound of mother's voice, Clara rose and went into the kitchen, chattering to her about the beautiful ocean and the waves. Lily didn't know what sort of magic had been in that glass, but it had changed Clara's life forever.

For weeks, Clara never left the ocean. With Lily she shared her secret wish to float away forever in those white-capped crests. She didn't understand how, but the glass walls she'd felt around her had softened like water, letting in the sounds, the touch of Lily's hand in hers—the call of the ocean. But Clara confessed she could get no closer to the waves than the edge of this beach and it made her sad.

As the summer waned, that sadness became a melancholy that sapped Clara's animation. Slowly like a low tide, Clara's connection ebbed away until Lily and her family lost Clara. By August, Clara had returned to her silent self marooned on the beige couch in the parlor. The float lay untouched in a bowl on the table.

Lily's frustration turned to anger as she carried the float in to Clara.

"Come on, Clara, take the float and we can go to the beach," she said, holding out the float. "You love the water!"

Clara's gaze didn't even move toward her.

"Clara, please—take the float. Let's go play, okay?"

Silence.

Thad ran into the parlor. "Iwee!" he squealed, unable to say 'Lily.' His eyes grew wide and he moved closer to Lily, his little index finger pointing. "Ball," he said.

"Go play, Thad," Lily snapped and turned back to Clara who hadn't even looked at her. "Clara, listen to me. I know you hear me."

"Ball," Thad repeated, his voice rising in a whine.

Tears streaked down Lily's face. "If you won't come out, I'm taking the float back."

"Have ball!" Thad shouted.

"Fine!" Lily cried and rushed over to the back door. She threw the float outside. It bumped down the path and rolled onto the beach.

"Ball!" Thad shouted again, his face twisting.

Lily ran out of the parlor and upstairs to her attic bedroom.

Lily's arthritis ached as she struggled to lean against the motel room's headboard.

"I didn't understand about Clara's autism and I didn't understand what the float was. I thought she was okay."

"So what was the float?" Samantha asked.

"Some of the local fishermen call them a mermaid's looking glass," Lily said, her voice quivering. "A short glimpse of what could be. Nothing more. What I thought was Clara's recovery was little more than an illusion. A cruel trick!"

Samantha sat up, her dark gaze intense. "What happened after you threw the float outside."

Tears rushed down Lily's face and she sucked in a breath. "What happened after that still haunts me."

The shrill scream launched Lily out of her bed. She raced downstairs to Ruth's frantic shouting.

"Thad? Thad, this isn't funny—where are you? Thad!"

Ruth grabbed Lily by the shoulders when she saw her on the stairs.

"Lily, is Thad with you?"

"No, why?"

"He's missing," she said, her voice strangling on the words.

"The last time I saw him," Lily said, rushing toward the parlor, "was in here with—"

The couch was empty.

She glanced at the back door. It stood ajar.

Cold fear pressed against Lily's chest.

The float. She'd thrown it outside and Thad saw her do it.

"Oh my God!" Lily screamed and bolted out the back door.

Running down the path, she tumbled over some rocks, picked herself up, and kept running until she reached the edge of the beach.

Little footprints tracked across the wet sand.

"Thad!" she shrieked, the wind burning her tear-soaked face. "Thad, it's Iwee! Please come out!"

She stumbled over something in the sand. Glancing down, she found the float, not even a chip or scratch on it, lying there in the sand.

"Thad!" Lily wailed.

On the edge of the surf, something dark tangled against a nearby tree stump.

Lily's screams brought Ruth and Phillip to the beach, Sophie and Mother not far behind. When Ruth saw the little footprints and the dark tangle around the driftwood, she went berserk.

"No! Oh, God—Thad! Thad!"

Phillip held her back. "No, you can't go out there," he shouted.

Ruth clawed frantically at him, screaming her son's name until she collapsed against Phillip.

Holding the float against her chest, Lily cried.

"Thad, I'm so sorry!"

The waves pounded the beach and all Lily could do was scream.

"Ball?"

At the sound of the inquisitive little voice, Lily jerked her head around. Sandy, soaked, and all smiles, Thad held out his little arms for the ball.

"Oh my God! Thad!" Lily threw her arms around him. "He's here!" she screamed.

Ruth fell twice when she tripped over her long skirts, but she swept Thad into her arms, smothering him with hugs and kisses.

He held onto the float in his chubby little arms. "Have ball," he said.

Lily's gaze fell back to the log and then she knew the rest of the story. She ran to Ruth and laid her hands on Thad's arms.

"Thad, were you out here alone?"

He shook his head and put his hand high over his head. "Water go boom. Cwara swim."

Lily brushed the tears from her old, old eyes. "Maybe Clara realized she could never go back to the place she'd left? Maybe she thought the float could bring her out again or maybe it was Thad? I'll never know the answer to that, but somehow, Clara found the courage to rise from the couch."

"She saved Thad's life, didn't she?" Samantha asked, sitting next to Lily on the same bed.

Lily nodded. "People on the beach saw the rogue wave hit the beach and the girl run in to save a little boy."

Samantha laid her hand on Lily's shoulder and squeezed. "But it wasn't the same Clara who ran onto that beach, Grandma. Before the mermaid's looking glass, she'd never touched the beach. And she wouldn't have done that without you."

"It was my fault that Clara died," Lily said, wincing. "If I hadn't thrown that float outside, Thad wouldn't have gone after it."

"And if you hadn't given the looking glass to Clara, she wouldn't have understood what it meant to feel. For a few weeks, Clara was free. And she chose to stay that way, Grandma."

Samantha was right. What kind of life would Clara had led back then? What would have happened to her after Mother and Daddy passed away? The glimpse in the looking glass had given her a choice. It was the best thing Lily could have done for her. And the best thing Lily could do for Clara was return the looking glass to the Pacific.

"It's time to send it back on its way," said Lily as she struggled up from the bed.

Bending slowly, deliberately, she scooped up the looking glass and moved toward the door.

"I'll get my shoes," said Samantha, springing up from the bed.

The chilly breeze was taut against Lily's cheeks as she walked down the stairs, down the sidewalk to the turnaround. She paused at the steps until she felt Samantha's arm on hers, urging her forward. She made no move to follow, as if understanding that Lily needed to do this alone.

Sand shifted beneath her tennis shoes as Lily moved toward the water's roar. The memory of Clara tangled in the driftwood was vivid in her tired mind as she approached the water's turbulent edge.

All these years, she'd hated this awful thing, blaming it and herself for Clara's death. But now, all she felt was grateful.

Heaving her arm back, Lily closed her eyes and tossed the mermaid's looking glass into the wild surf. Waves crashed and surged against the hard-packed sand, and she almost missed the musical laugh above the rush.

Lily opened her eyes, searching for the warm sound as her gaze traveled across the empty beach front.

"Clara?" she called.

Again, that musical laugh rose above the waves, peeling away the years and bringing cold tears to Lily's eyes.

"I'm so sorry—it was all my fault!" she shouted. Her heart ached as she stepped closer to the waves.

A gray-green fin arched through the steely waters, disappearing into the foam and kelp.

Like the echo of wind chimes, Clara's laughter rose on the surf. "You freed me," Clara's voice singsonged. "Thank you."

Again, the arch of a fin and the musical echo of "thank you" hung in the air as the mermaid's looking glass rolled onto the beach. Lily struggled against her stiff limbs to pick up the float, but Samantha was beside her, pressing the float into her hands.

Within the misty glass, Clara's doe-eyed dark-haired gaze stared back, a smile on her nine-year-old lips. Then she swam toward deep waters, the faint graceful arc of a fluke behind her.

It hadn't been a curse, giving only a cruel glimpse of what could have been. It had transformed Clara! Lily kissed the float and threw it back into the waves. At last, she and Clara were both free.

NIGHTWEAVER

The shuttle whispered across the woolen warp strands, green as evergreens, and wefted crimson fibers into the cloth that poked at Muriel's belly. The scent of dry wool clung to her face like a mask as she smoothed the heavy fabric with an aching hand. Two generations intertwined the green and red serpent's knot. It was nearly finished after all this time. She glanced back at Himself, quilts pulled tight across him, skin pale, tousles of thinning black waves showing above the patchwork roses. Wind ached around the walls of the cottage, rustling the thatched roof and copper pans hanging over the hearth as it moaned on its way across the moors.

Amber candlelight flickered with every pass of the shuttle, beams and pedals squeaking as she raised and lowered the warp. This cloth had begun with her mother, the knotted design born on a lonely winter moor night when the heather frosted and the stones turned to hunks of gray ice. Tonight, she felt in the company of the weavers who had gone before her, weaving life on this loom. The company was welcome; it was a long, lonely stretch until dawn.

She sighed at the vanishing skein of crimson flax. She needed more madder dye for the pattern. Himself needed her to finish, otherwise it would be another long winter.

Muriel laid down the shuttle and shuffled over to the wooden bed. Leaning down, she patted Himself on the shoulder and kissed his cheek.

"I'll be back before dawn," she spoke as she slid into a black cloak, thin white fingers thrust into the sleeves.

After pulling her traveling satchel from beneath the cupboard, she flicked her flaxen hair into the hood and went out into the night.

Something howled across the moors tonight as her boots crunched through the long grasses. She glanced around at the swaying trees, darkness thick like wool. Perhaps a lone hellhound fearing the icy air and the roar of the winds? Cold enough to choke the life from the fiercest demon. Many shades of undead walked these moors at night, especially with the longest night approaching. She wrapped the cloak tighter about her middle and pulled a small bundle of sheepskin from her pocket. Quickly, she wrapped her sore fingers in the soft skin, the night mist frosty and ashen. Even the wind smelled of ice and soon-coming snow.

Himself needed her to finish tonight.

The hard path wound through a clearing. That's when the rustle began, soft like a rabbit's scamper. Muriel's pace quickened. She slid her right hand out of the sheepskin and felt for the wooden stake wedged into her other pocket. Her tired fingers wrapped around it.

Abruptly, the howl strangled in mid-bay and fell silent. She shivered. Even hellhounds feared the undead.

A mournful wail reverberated across the moors, the lap of water touching her ears. The sound rolled up into layers like whispers in a crypt and dissipated into the frost. She clutched the stake, the scrape of branches puncturing the lament.

It sounded closer now.

Footsteps echoed on the path behind her. A bird screeched. She paused, breath frosting in icy puffs.

The boot-sounds stopped, matching her step. She glanced behind, the heaviness of the cold against her pale cheeks. No one.

Ahead, the silvery moon illuminated the path away from the moors, toward the plains and one of the stone circles. When brush crackled again, she ran toward the path.

It was too late in the season for most of the Druidic rituals, the moors too stark and the moon too cold. Except for their vigil on the longest night of darkness. That would come soon, but not tonight. The circle of stones would be empty.

Again, the dull thunk of boots touched her ears and she fled down the path until the shadows pooled like the simmering elder bark she used for black dye. The indigo sky was crisp and nearly starless as the ancient forest finally receded from the plains ahead and the circle's power. Mist hung like mourner's veils across the plains that stretched an eternity's length to the circle. She had to reach it.

Brush snapped. A bird took flight. Mist rippled closer.

Muriel drew an icy breath and dashed toward the stones. As she stepped into the center of the circle, she saw the sacrificial stones splotched ruddy brown. Dried, faded blood. It had been some time since the Druids had been here.

A flock of birds clattered out of the trees and fluttered low overhead. With a hand still on the stake, she glanced around, watching for the approach of something she only felt in the sudden evening stillness.

She eased her satchel onto the ground, watching the plains from all sides.

Off to her right, the mist billowed and began to coalesce. From it stepped a brown-haired young man. He moved toward her, the trees at his back. His long, angular face, pale as the winter moon, hungered, frost-blue eyes leering.

He moved like a nobleman, his steps steady and sure. She stood motionless as he approached. He drew closer, his light brown hair soft and smooth against his forehead. As he reached the outermost stone, the hint of fangs glinted at his mouth.

Muriel backed away until she felt the sacrificial stone at her back, chilling her through her cloak.

"Shouldn't you be home in bed?" the man asked, his voice like ebony silk. He leered at her again.

She gazed into the light eyes, the fangs white as a child's headstone and smiled. "I needed more madder for my weaving," she answered in a husky voice, her breath misting.

"Stone circles are even more dangerous than the moors, dear young lady."

She took a step backward. Couldn't. "Yes, there is danger here."

"Especially for maidens unfortunate enough to visit them at night."

He moved closer, a bony hand reaching out to her. He took her gently by the shoulders. She closed her eyes, feeling his warmth through the cloak as it radiated across her skin. He had just fed on something, she thought, or someone. She smelled the metallic, warm scent of dried blood mix with the wool of his cloak.

His eyes waxed with pleasure as his hands slid down her arms and beneath her cloak. His lips pressed against hers and she felt his need. It ached through him until she felt it tremble through her own body. She thrust her head back and gasped as he kissed across her chin and down her neck. His lips parted to embrace her neck, fangs visible and she leaned in to him, the sheepskin falling away from her hands.

Even when she plunged the stake through his back, into his heart, she embraced him, feeling the warm blood of his body against hers until she felt his aching need ebb. His voice gurgled then hissed as he struggled to pull away, but she thrust the stake harder until she felt him weaken . His knees buckled and he sank to her feet. Finally, the life-force receded and he fell motionless against the ground. Releasing his arm, she reached into her satchel and removed her milk jar.

It was only about two hours before dawn when Muriel returned home. She hung her cloak on the wall near the hearth and plucked the skeins of ivory flax from the wall. She dipped them lovingly into her blood-filled milk jar until the skeins sparkled crimson and left them to dry beside the hearth. With a yawn, she returned to her loom, feeling her fellow weavers close as the shuttle fit into her palm. Wind swept across the cottage as she finished off the remaining strand of crimson. Once again, something on the moors wailed, but she let the sound slip away as she studied the inter-twining knot pattern that twisted and swerved across the evergreen background. Interconnected as the lifeblood of her ancestors.

She would try to finish it again tomorrow night, now that she had more crimson flax.

Rising from the chair, she went to Himself and sat down on the bed beside him. She straightened the quilt then turned it down. A russet hole encircled with dried blood gaped in his faded white shirt, revealing a puncture in the powdery blue-white skin, so near his heart. Thank the moors that the villager's stake had missed its target.

She had dyed her first skein of flax with that man's blood—only out of spite—for a mortal's blood was nothing more than coloring for the pattern. It would take much undead blood to complete the Pattern of Life upon Himself's shroud to restore him, but she would finish what her mother had started. Mother had taught her the intricacies of the pattern as well as the art of weaving and she would finish the serpent's knot shroud for her father. Himself would be pleased.

She smiled at him, feeling her fangs press softly against her lips. Smudging a bit of dried blood from the corner of her mouth, she rose, the lament of the wind rushing across the shutters. It was a comforting sound. When the cloth was finished, the Pattern would restore him. Until then, there were many undead walking the moors. The nights were long and the Druidic circles were close enough to shroud her again. She would have more than enough dye before the madder bloomed again in the spring.

WHISPERS

Sinners and saints walk through the midnight snows surrounding St. Marie. I stand in the church foyer and listen as their whispers echo in the crunch of snow, the hush of breath. Their footprints mingle with those of the living.

Candles, lit in remembrance of lost loved ones, flutter amber across the nave, casting long shadows through the foyer and into the somber night. I take a stiff drink and put the small bottle back in my torn pocket, waiting for the sharp draught to settle in my stomach. Then I limp into the nave.

Silence wraps around me like wool and I can't breathe. I tug at the top button of my blue uniform shirt where a tie used to be and finally, my breath returns. I sigh, thinking of my tie and uniform jacket lying in a trash can. Let them burden someone else now. I no longer have a use for them. Like Laurie no longer had a use for me. I smooth the sleeve of my disheveled shirt and slide into the last pew. The church is full, but I can't look at their faces.

Already, the flutter begins in the entry way behind me. A rustle of wings that mixes with the lingering whispers. They are razors in my ears.

Incense mingles with the bitter scent of scotch as altar boys, dressed in starched red and white robes, file down the aisle misting the nave with purifying incense rich in antiquity and myrrh. It washes over me and I want to laugh. Only fire purifies filth.

I reach for my bottle again, but the wings sound closer now. Wind hisses against my neck. My hand shakes and I pull it away from my pocket. O Holy Night sounds through the church and my gaze rises to the angels resting in the rafters. Angels of Death. There is sternness in their beauty, retribution in their praying hands, death in their flowing robes. I clasp my hands together and tears flow from a long dry well as I call to the angels. They wait in silence for my confession.

A rush of wind whips through the church as the door opens. Snow crunches and someone else steps inside. A woman sits in the pew across from me. I turn away, curling into myself. I can't look. I can't bear to see what I've done to her and the others.

The beating of wings flutters against the organ music. The melody bores into my bones and resonates in my stomach. I know I have to look at the woman. I have to face her.

Slowly, I steal a glance. Her face, half-burned, stares straight ahead. Her torn, bloody uniform is blackened, pantyhose shredded, legs bleeding. She was barely twenty-two. This was her second week on the job. I turn away again, my stomach clenching.

"My life is over," she whispers as the congregation sings "Fall on your knees . . . O hear the angel voices."

And I took it.

My heart twists, the ache unbearable. I bow my head, but am distracted by the young man across from me who waves with the stump of a right hand. The empty socket where an eye had been turns toward me and his whispers mingle with the young woman's. He was nineteen and going home for Christmas.

Above me, wings murmur as an angel takes flight.

"Nothing changes, does it, David?"

That voice is so painfully familiar that my chest aches. I turn.

Laurie stands in the aisle, no hint of the anger and hopelessness that sent her out of my life six weeks ago. Her thick blond hair is feathered and neatly arranged, pink sweater and black jeans pristine. God, she looks good. I stand painfully.

"Laurie . . . how—?"

"You summoned me," she says and leans against the pew,

motioning toward the parishioners. "Like you summoned the rest of them. We have a lot in common."

I turn. A family of four sits three pews in front of me. The two children turn like rag dolls, limbs flopping, heads limp on their necks. Their mouths stretch into broken smiles, their faces wrecked. They were going to their grandmother's house in Grand Rapids.

"I'm sorry!" I shout. "I'm so sorry!" My voice rises in layers, the sound falling back onto itself until the words are lost.

The congregation turns to stare, one hundred and sixty people with shattered faces and mangled bodies. I press my face into my hands and sobs erupt.

"Are you sorry, David?"

Laurie's tone is caustic, a side I had forgotten. So many things about her have grown fuzzy. The four years I spent with her were a lifetime ago. I've left behind so much.

"Of course I'm sorry!" I scream and hobble toward her. "Do you think I wanted this?"

She shakes her head. "Like the night you nearly wrapped my new car around a tree? You didn't understand then and you don't understand now."

I bow my head and her hand smoothes my damp, tangled hair. Her hand has a ghostly lightness that is more wind than substance. I can't remember how her touch feels. Like my life, like these moments I can't quite face.

"I know why you've brought us here, David, but we aren't the ones who can absolve you." She looks toward the ceiling.

Clouds of incense collect in the indigo blackness above. Is it ceiling or sky? I can't tell anymore.

"Even this place can't absolve you."

I gaze at the stained glass windows lining the ornate oak walls. Green and amber lights wink, occasionally washing red. I clench my eyes closed. I don't want to see beyond the confines of those windows, of this church.

Laurie's hand slides into my shirt pocket. She takes the small travel bottle and holds it out to me. I wince, unwilling to remember where I'd gotten it.

"You never knew how to be happy. You used me, like you use this, to make you happy."

"I never used you!" I shout. "I loved you!"

"You consumed me, David! You burned me out day by day until I had no identity, nothing left to give. But you kept taking with promises that became lies."

My bottom lip quivers. "I know, I know."

Her hand slides to my cheek, cupping it. "God, David—don't you realize what you've done?"

The whispers grow sharper, the music louder. I pull away, my hands shaking as I press them to my ears. No, I can't remember it all. I can't.

"You've got to face it, David. It's your only chance. You're drowning."

Her arms enfold me. Only for an instant, I feel her warm touch against my skin. Tears flood my cheeks as the touch fades.

She drops the bottle on the floor and moves toward the church door.

"Laurie, wait! Laurie!"

A young woman rises from the pew and stumbles toward me. Her chiseled chin is cut and bleeding down the front of her uniform. The woman reaches for me, sadness in her eyes. I scramble to take her hands, but they slip beneath my unsteady grasp.

She touches my face and whispers, "How could you do this to us? We trusted you."

I fall to my knees. My soul aches and my voice chokes.

Her voice is sharp. "We trusted you."

Her bloody fingers move to the pilot's wings on my shirt. She tears off the wings, dropping them in my hands.

I rock back and forth, staring at the bloodied wings. I caused this. I feel it now. For a moment, the church blurs.

Outside, ambulances screech by, drowning out the music and the whispers and the wings. Through the stained glass, the red lights whip past, mingling with the wink of green and amber.

I fall backward as rich soprano notes, the singing of angels, fill the emptiness. My broken legs ache and I can't feel my right arm.

Rafters swirl above me, angels and incense trails spinning, dead faces and smoking cockpit whirling into a red and white haze. Stained glass falls away.

Outside the cockpit, ambulance lights flutter red across the snowy runway, casting long shadows into the somber night. The beating of helicopter blades hisses behind me, airlifting survivors out of the snow-covered debris.

Above me, the cockpit is laid open like a tin can. Through the tear, cold stars appear overhead. Snow drifts down on the cockpit floor, melting against the sparking control panel.

"I caused this," I mutter. "Laurie's right."

A young flight attendant cowers beside me, her face half-burned. Her blackened uniform and shredded, her pantyhose drip with blood.

"Why?" she screeches. "Why did you do this?"

Through the open cabin door, I see them all, all one hundred and sixty people looking almost asleep—except for their whispers. I clutch my head. Oh, God, the whispers!

From a police officer's radio, O Holy Night rises above the flutter of wings, the whispers in the crunching snow. Sinners and saints walk through the midnight snows surrounding Sault Sainte Marie.

Someone cuts away my jacket and tie, tossing them aside. A blur of red and white files down the cabin aisle, fire extinguishers misting the stillness, paramedics and firefighters race.

So many times I promised Laurie I'd stop drinking, so she wouldn't leave and, dear God, I tried. But the layovers got too lonely and my suitcase grew too heavy.

A rag doll lies in the aisle near the cockpit door. I can't look past it at the little girl it had once belonged to, the little girl going to Grand Rapids to see her grandmother. Oh, God, the whispers! What have I done? I open my mouth to scream, but nothing escapes the silence inside me.

Something glints in the red haze. One of those deadly little scotch bottles rocks back and forth, a pendulum swinging toward me. I try to ignore the sharp, raw rhythm. For once in my life I try. But I can't help myself. I reach for it.

"Fall on your knees," the heavenly chorus warbles above the whispers.

The green numbers of my watch glare back at me: 12:12 am. Christmas Day.

"O hear the angel voices . . . "

I stare at the slumped figure of the now-silent flight attendant. She was twenty-two. She'd been at the job for two weeks.

I pour out the scotch, watch it trickle onto the floor toward the control panel. Flames whisper through the cockpit as the Angel of Death's wings flutter across my face. It is the last whisper and I welcome it.

SAFE AS THE DARK

Scalding light hung at the edge of his vision. Coby Barnes blinked and the world careened toward him from the dark behind his eyes. For a moment, he didn't feel his arms, didn't feel his legs, not even the self-inflicted gunshot wound to his head.

His chest heaved with breath and it startled him. He remembered the shotgun blast and taking his last breath. Warm, sticky blood clung to the side of his face. He tried to feel his hands, wondering if he still clutched the shotgun, but couldn't. Gasping, he opened his eyes. He looked past the grim faces hovering over him and realized he was still at the school. But this hadn't been part of the game. Five body bags—his former classmates—slipped past as they laid him on a gurney. Then it hit him. He was still alive.

He glanced to his side and saw the other two boys who'd come inside with him. A bloodied sheet covered Rick's body, the red blotch widening. Rick's stiff, bloody hand clutched the sawed off shotgun that lay beside him. Rick looked like the dead guys in his Target Assault game. Or one of those FirstLook clips on the net where they showed crime scenes live and unedited. Rick would have liked that. Turner lay beside Rick, an IV in his arm.

"We got them before they could get us, Coby," said Turner, grinning. "Said they hated us, that we didn't belong in McKinley High. Now, who doesn't belong here." A deep laugh rattled through Turner's chest, but it died on his lips.

A police officer roughly carted Turner toward the speck of light at the end of the dark hallway.

Another body bag slipped past. Across from him, a woman hugged the wall and sobbed. Footsteps ticked down the hallway. The cloying scent of stale blood mixed with soured sweat and sulfur. In the distance, a voice wailed. Policemen corded off hallways and led huddles of people out of the school.

Coby hadn't expected to survive the assault. Turner had planned it for months, how they'd die at the end and all. They'd practiced and everything. This wasn't supposed to happen. The rage swelled in his chest, making his fists ache to hit something.

A pale-faced police officer snapped a handcuff around Coby's wrist and attached the other end to the gurney. Maybe now people wouldn't mess with him? Maybe now they'd see that he wouldn't take their insults?

A paramedic in light blue scrubs leaned over him, a gold nameplate pinned to his white lab coat: Plexus Juvenile Correctional Facility. The man wore gold-rimmed glasses and looked about thirty.

"Coby Barnes," spoke the police officer beside him. "You are charged in the shooting deaths of six McKinley High School students." The police officer mumbled off a list of his rights. "You are remanded to the Plexus Juvenile Correctional Facility where you will remain until your trial date is set."

Something pressed into the crook of his arm and things got fuzzy.

A sheet was thrown across him as the gurney lurched forward and squeaked toward the speck of light.

Coby regained consciousness in a police van en-route to the Plexus Juvenile Correctional Facility along with his buddies, Turner and Rick. He had no idea how much time had passed, but the wound on his head had been stitched up and no longer hurt. Turner sat beside him, smug as he fingered his dirty blond goatee. His stringy blond hair, two shades lighter than his goatee, hung in his eyes, but in those eyes, Coby saw that familiar "we showed those bastards" look. Rick sat on the other side of Turner, grinning, his curly black hair smashed against his head. He was tall and looked twenty pounds underweight.

"It was just like Target Assault, wasn't it, Coby?" Turner said, grinning at him from across the dim-lit van.

Coby nodded. "Yeah, Turner. It was just like you said."

"Remember, in the game, when our squad's in the caverns. You and me and Rick gunning for our targets."

"I always get killed there," Rick said with a sigh. "I never could get through there without dying."

Turner's gaze centered on Coby. "Remember, Coby? Just you and me in the cavern, watching each other's backs and fragging anything that moved. We made a good team, you and me."

"Yeah, we made a good team," said Coby with a smile. Then he gazed down at the chains and it all felt confused somehow. He sighed, trying to separate the cavern's deathmatch with the school shooting, but they overlapped in his head. Turner kept talking, describing other parts of Target Assault. Coby settled back in the van and listened. It took his mind off where they were headed.

Coby had expected an isolated complex somewhere, but the van drove north toward Chicago. As they approached the south side with its abandoned factories and tall, crumbling brick buildings, Coby got nervous. The abandoned, decaying buildings covered miles of abandoned city blocks, sidewalks cracked and windows smashed. The smell of burnt rubber and sewage hung in the air, making Coby gag. In his government studies class, Coby remembered some ozone or air pollution act where the government closed a bunch of factories, leaving big sections of city blocks abandoned. The van turned a corner and stopped in front of a massive, steel gate. One of the officers leaned out the van window and slid an access card through a reader near the gate. The street vibrated as the gate hummed open and the van slipped inside.

Coby, Turner, and Rick, shackled in wrist and ankle chains, were herded out of the van and into a small room. One of the officers typed in some codes on a recessed panel on the wall. The wall slid open, revealing a long hallway. Coby's chains clacked down the long hallway, lights snapping on every few feet. His breath quickened and he glanced over at Turner. The sneer had slid from his face.

"You know anything about this place, Coby?" Turner demanded.

Coby shook his head. "I never heard of it."

Turner always had to be in charge. He always had an opinion, too and a reason for doing anything. Coby, Turner, and Rick had played Target Assault over the net for years, so he was used to Turner's style. They'd always hung around together, smoking on the school's loading dock behind the cafeteria. That's where all the outsiders hung out, the only place in school where they could be themselves and not be ridiculed. He'd met Turner and Rick there. Shortly after, they started playing Target Assault.

In their senior year, Turner wanted to make things special. That's when he came up with the school version of the game. They'd play the kamikaze deathmatch and pay those snobby little bastards back for treating them like scum.

"This place looks like the opening screen for kamikaze deathmatch," Turner said, laughing.

It kind of did look like that opening screen. Coby could almost feel the joystick action as his Target Assault character surged around corners, rifle raised, ready to take down anything that moved. He remembered yesterday afternoon in the school when they'd gone in with rifles. Turner had gotten them from his uncle's den. How different that rifle felt in his hands than a joystick.

At the end of the hallway was another gate. Coby peered through it, seeing the overcast sky and the crumbling buildings. This didn't make any sense. Why had they come through a gate that led no where?

On the right-hand side of the gate was another door. A man in a gray suit, crisp white shirt, and pale yellow tie stepped out of an office. He wore a gold name badge that Coby couldn't read, but the title 'Warden' was in thick black letters. Stocky and balding, he reeked of too much after-shave and his suit smelled of money.

"Good morning, gentlemen," said the man as he moved toward the gate. He motioned toward the three officers who removed

Coby's ankle and wrist chains. Next, they removed Turner's chains then Rick's. "You'll go into the Block."

"The Block? What the hell's the block?" Turner demanded.

The man seemed unconcerned with Turner's objection. "It's a new facility for violent Juvenile offenders."

"Hey, I know my rights and you can't do this!" shouted Turner. "I got a right to a trial and an attorney!"

The warden stepped closer. "You three gave up your rights when you open-fired on your classmates. Your families think you died in the school attack."

"But you can't do this!" Turner shouted, rushing toward the warden.

One of the officers jerked Turner back by the hair as the Warden slid an access card through a reader on the wall. The massive gate slid open into the city block.

Yellow grid lines pulsed across the sky and around the buildings. It made the hairs on Coby's arm bristle. They pulsed like a flare and then faded into the overcast sky as the gate behind them closed. Turner bolted across the broken sidewalk and lunged headlong, but a flash of sparks threw him several feet backward. He slammed into the pavement, dazed, for a moment, but then he rose from the ground.

"What the hell is this place?" Turner demanded, squinting at the burned out buildings. "Help me up."

Coby and Rick rushed to help him to his feet.

"Are they just going to leave us in here forever?" Rick demanded.

Coby stared at the layout. A single city block with half a dozen, red-brick buildings on each side of one lonely street that stretched into the hazy distance. The street ended abruptly at a brick wall. The whup, whup of a fan echoed through the quiet street. He couldn't see where the fan noise was coming from, but he heard it in the quiet. The street's pavement was old and broken, potholes and grass pushing up through the weakening surface. Sidewalks lined both sides of the street. A crumpled Budweiser can lay in the gutter beside a shattered, amber bottle and wet paper sack. The smell of old asphalt and garbage hung in the air.

On the edge of his vision, Coby saw movement. He jerked his head around, catching a glimpse of orange fade into the nearest brick building to his left. A sick feeling hung in the pit of his stomach. They weren't alone in here.

From a second story window, bullets pounded the dry patch of grass. Rick's body lurched, the dull whump of the impacts driving him backward until he collapsed onto the sidewalk. He tried to scream, but it gurgled in his throat.

"Yeah! Got a new one!" shouted an excited voice from a second floor window.

Coby and Turner ran toward the nearest building on their right, throwing themselves in the doorway as bullets ripped across the brick face.

The building was dark, broken furniture and dust littering the floor as they plunged inside. It smelled musty. A room off to the left opened into a bay window and a stone fireplace. Straight ahead, a rickety staircase led to a second floor.

Coby ran into the room on the left and crouched in one of the bay windows. His chest heaved. This wasn't cool. He glanced at Turner who knelt beside him. He hadn't expected the excited look on Turner's face or the rifles on the floor of the building.

"It's pay back time," Turner said, grinning. "Like in the deathmatch cavern."

Turner ran to the doorway and waved an arm. When a shot zinged through the doorway, Turner fired the rifle. A scream came from the second floor, a flash of orange tumbling through the window. Coby glanced out the window. Across the street, a young man in orange lay face down in the reddening grass.

Grinning, Turner hefted the rifle onto his shoulder. "This is like playing Target Assault, man! Come on, Coby! You and me! Grab a rifle!" He let out a whoop and ran out into the street, firing off shots. Coby snatched one of the rifles and followed. To him, this wasn't at all like Target Assault.

All through the day, gun fire echoed through the street, behind the buildings. Coby spent the day scoping out shooters, Turner leading the way. Toward the end of the day, Coby felt tired and returned to the building where they'd found the rifles. As it was getting dark, Turner showed up with two orange-suited prisoners. They walked slowly, hands on top of their heads.

"Coby!" Turner shouted, shoving his two prisoners into the building. "Check this out."

Coby slipped out from behind a pile of broken crates and scowled at Turner. He didn't say anything though. Turner always knew what he was doing.

"This is so much better than Target Assault," he said with a laugh and poked one of his prisoners in the back, a thin, chestnut-haired young man who looked gaunt and tired. "Better than McKinley High, too!" He nudged his other orange-suited prisoner, taller, stockier with dark hair. He had another rifle in his hand and tossed it to Coby who caught it. "How many of us are in here?"

"In the Block?" The taller one shrugged. "Depends on who's shooting and the time of day."

Turner kicked him and he fell to his knees. "What do you mean by that?"

"Every twelve hours, there's a blackout because they reset the security grid. It's pitch black in here for five hours. That's all I know. That's when the medbots come in and treat anybody who's hurt and bring in the food."

Coby realized he hadn't even thought about Rick who lay dead near the gate. All of this just seemed so unreal. Like watching the school kids fall in the hallways as Turner shot them. All of it seemed so unreal. He gripped the beaten up rifle.

"What happens to people who die in here?" Coby asked.

"Sometimes, the medbots can revive them," said the gaunt teenager, his bangs hanging in his eyes. "They carry off the bodies when they fall. Sometimes, after the blackouts, they're brought back."

He hoped Rick would be okay tomorrow, not sure what that suddenly mattered? It hadn't in the school. Not even when he put the shotgun to his own head. "How long until the next blackout?" Coby asked.

Turner glared at him. "Hey, I ask the questions. You're my second, remember?"

Coby nodded at him. He'd always played captain to Turner's major. Rick had always been first lieutenant and Coby wondered if Turner had even thought about Rick. Turner poked at the taller teenager. "So, when's the next blackout?"

"It's been several hours," he answered in a stiff voice. "It'll probably be soon, I guess. I don't know."

Grinning, Turner let the rifle rest against his right shoulder. "If you, two take me to your ammo stash, I'll let you live. With Rick dead, I've got openings."

The two teenagers nodded. "Okay. We haven't hooked up with any of the outfits," said the one with the bangs.

"Move out then. Come on, Coby. Watch my back."

With hands on their heads, the two teenagers led them up the stairs of the building and to a room at the top of the stairs. The harsh light from a bare bulb shadowed an open crate of shotgun shells. Turner dipped his fingers into the shells and grabbed handfuls, shoving them in his pockets. Coby filled his pockets, too. Shots rang out in the street again and they clamored downstairs to wait for the first blackout.

The world seemed to go away entirely when the blackout arrived. A soupy darkness enveloped the Block. All the buildings went dark and silent. Footsteps skittered across the pavement outside, a shrill, frightened whisper fading. Coby huddled beside one of the broken bay windows, clutching the rifle to his chest. Movement scraped the floor behind him.

"Turner?"

No answer. Something smacked against the floor.

"Turner!"

Somebody else was in the room with him and Turner. The gang across the street! He had to get out of here.

Panicked, Coby lurched up from the floor and out the broken bay window. He hit the grass with a thud. Terror gripped him and he was barely able to breathe. He rolled against the building, the brick rough against his cheek as he gazed across the street. But the black-ness was too thick.

Something slammed against the building. Rifle fire, he quickly realized. Scrambling to his feet, his arm aching, Coby ran toward the street. Above the echoes of his footfalls rose the distant whup, whup sound of a fan. Blue-white flashes pulsed through the dark-ness as he made his way toward the fan.

Soon the dull sounds of rifle fire fell away. He ran harder until he reached a massive fan embedded in a brick wall. It was four feet tall and spun slowly behind a screen. The blades whispered softly in the darkness, the blue-white flashes like cameras. He peered into the screen. Through the fan, he saw a park. Floodlights swelled, catching the bronze image of a little girl holding a foal. The statue stood in the middle of a fountain and the movement of the fan seemed to almost animate the girl.

Far down the street, shouts erupted. More shots fired. A scream. Footsteps pounded. He gasped for air as he pressed his back to the brick wall, desperate to hide himself from the gun fire. Were they coming for him? He raised the rifle to his shoulder. Pain sliced through his arm. Only then did he realize that he'd been shot.

Part of the brick wall shifted and something small and cylindrical rolled out. He jumped, shuffling back, but something cold touched his aching arm. A bandage pressed against the ache and Coby real-ized it was a medbot tending his arm. Whatever it was soothed the pain, making Coby a little groggy.

As he watched the spark of rifle fire down the street, he felt angry at the shooters. Didn't they ever stop? This didn't feel much like a game anymore. He leaned his head against the brick wall, the fleeting images of the girl and her foal and the gentle whup, whup of the fan making the dark feel safe.

In five hours, the blackout ended. Slowly, the darkness lightened to a dull gray. Coby awoke to find bread, cheese, and water in a basket at his feet. He devoured the food and drank the water, leaving the empty containers beside the wall. His arm was stiff, but the sharp ache where the bullet had grazed his flesh was gone. He raced across the street as gunfire shattered the silence. All around him, the yellowish glow of the security grid flared to life and then faded to gray. He ducked behind trashcans and around buildings until he reached the first building nearest the gate, the one he and Turner had claimed.

When he shoved through the half-open door, Turner grabbed him and threw him to the ground. A rifle barrel pressed into his cheek.

"Don't shoot, it's me, Coby!"

Turner sighed and pulled back his rifle. Coby scrambled to his feet. Turner's orange scrubs were blood-spattered and torn. He walked with a limp, but otherwise seemed fine.

"Where were you?" Turner asked. "I thought you'd turned into a weenie and ran."

Coby sighed and ran his hand through his dark hair. "When the blackout hit, someone fired at the window. I jumped out and just started running until I lost the shooter."

Turner rolled his eyes and motioned him into the big room. Four other prisoners loaded rifles. They gave him a cursory look and returned to loading the rifles.

"What's going on?"

"There's a gang of prisoners across the street who tried to kill us last night, so we're going to surprise them."

"Surprise them?" Coby squawked.

"They said we don't belong here, so they're trying to kill us off. Bastards think they run the place, so we're going to get them before they get us."

That conversation sounded so familiar. So many times over a pack of Merits, Turner had raged about how the kids at McKinley hated them, wanted them to die. That they didn't belong in the school. So many times, Turner said they should get the bastards first. That's what got him and Turner in this place.

"Hey, Coby! Remember that one move we used to do in the cavern sequence? The one where one of us flushed out the monsters and the other one mowed 'em down as they came out? Remember, you and me?"

"Yeah, I remember." He had never realized how much Turner droned on about games before. Coby glanced around again, hoping to see Rick among the other orange suits. "Did Rick come back this morning?"

Turner looked at him like he was an idiot. "Who the hell cares, man! I'm talking about a cool deathmatch here. Us and them." A wary look spread across Turner's face. "You're in, aren't you?"

Coby nodded. What choice did he have? "Yeah, I'm in."

For days, Turner plotted ways to attack the building across the street. No matter how they approached the building, the moment they slipped inside, the shoot out turned into a stalemate. And every time, the other orange-suits retreated to the second floor and shot through holes in the ceiling, forcing Turner to call a retreat.

Whenever the blackouts came, Coby slipped away. He felt safer by the fan. Calmer. Through the fan, he studied the glistening bronze statue of the girl loving her foal, cradling it so tightly. Like it was her own child.

Reminded him of his sister's farm and the little tan calf he used to show in 4-H Club. The little calf had followed him around the fence, through mud puddles, always hurrying to keep up. Coby liked how the little guy had followed him around, like he was something special. By the end of the summer, the calf had grown a lot and done well at the state fair. Then, just before school started, he visited his sister. When he went out to the pasture, only a few red and white cows grazed. The little tan calf was gone. They'd sold him to market, his sister had said. Coby never went back after that.

His chest tightened and he stared at the girl and the foal. How would she have felt if someone had sold it to market or shot it to death? He felt sick as he laid his head against his rifle and slept.

Coby lost track of the days and how many blackouts there had been. And how many times Turner had led them across the street to attack the other group of prisoners. Turner relished every moment he held that rifle. Shooting it excited him. Coby dragged his rifle behind him, letting the rifle butt scuff against the pavement. The others shined their weapons until they gleamed, but Coby shoved his into a corner, only picking it up when Turner gave the signal to attack.

And this day was no different than the last one. Another gray, lifeless morning began as they charged across the street in a line. Bullets streaked past, catching the young man beside Coby. The young man clutched his side and doubled over. Coby grabbed his arm and pulled him out of the way, behind a green trash bin that stood near the building.

The young man's eyes were glazed and from behind the trash bin, he fired at the building.

"What are you doing? Stay down!" Coby shouted. "You want to get yourself killed?"

The young man looked through him and then reloaded his rifle.

Coby slumped against the trash bin, those words hitting him hard. He thought about the high school and the body bags now. It had been a game to him, to all of them. He shuddered. A good time.

The young man jumped up and shot at the building again. Then he fell to his knees as a hail of bullets pounded into the trash bin. Coby covered his ears, the dull impacts reminding him of the kids that Turner had shot. He shivered. He'd have followed Turner anywhere. He talked so big and how they all hated him. Coby, Rick, all of them outcasts. Just like the guys in this building. Who'd be next after them?

Turner cackled and fired wildly at the windows.

Above them, windows rained bullets. Coby glared at Turner. He was tired of following.

"Let's get out of here!" Coby shouted, grabbing the young man's arm beside him. "Back across the street! Now!"

He hauled the young man to his feet and across the street. The others followed.

"Damn you, Coby—stop! Stop!"

Coby ignored Turner's enraged shouts as he led the others back into the building.

"That was cool!" one of them said, grinning as he waved the rifle around.

Turner barreled through the doorway and lunged at Coby, striking him in the chest. "Why'd you call a retreat? Damn you, I'm leading this outfit!"

Coby slammed him against the wall. "This isn't a game!" he shouted and pounded the wall with his fist. "Six people are dead because of us! Don't you get that?" He let Turner go and turned away.

"But they made our lives miserable. They deserved to die. Like these guys. It's the same thing."

He turned. "For what? Calling us names?" He bit his lip and stared up at the torn rafters above him. "We'd have graduated in a few months—and we'd have never seen them again. We wouldn't be here now." Coby turned to the others. "You don't have to keep shooting at those guys across the street. You don't have to shoot at all."

A cold look spread across Turner's face. "You trying to take over, Coby?"

"Not me, man." he said. "I don't want any part of this anymore."

He moved past Turner toward the door.

"You're just like them," said Turner.

Coby kept walking. That's what tore at him most. He *was* just like them.

In six hours, the security grid went dark, resetting itself. Coby stashed himself underneath some rusted machinery and slept for a few hours. He awoke to darkness and slipped through the soupy blackness toward the fan. For a long time, he huddled against the wall and stared at the statue through fan slats. Seeing the girl cradling her foal made his eyes fill with tears. He hadn't cried for a very long time.

Could he get through here before everything came online again? Coby let the rifle fall against the wall as he pried at the screen, but something poked him in the back.

"Trying to escape, Coby?" Turner asked.

Coby turned, unable to see Turner. He was a faint presence in the darkness.

"What do you want, Turner?"

"You remember that one deathmatch, Coby, you and me against

a whole platoon of guys," said Turner in a slow voice. He sounded strange. "The one in the cavern."

"Yeah, I remember," Coby said, an edge in his voice.

"You remember how we finished off the computer guys, but then it was you and me left in that cavern."

The hair on Coby's neck bristled. He nodded. "We played that one a few weeks ago."

The flash of yellow flickered around him, the security grid shuddering to life. The blackout was over.

He and Turner stared into each other's eyes now. "It was you and me, Turner. In the school. And like now. Remember?"

Coby nodded. He'd actually laughed as they'd roamed McKinley's halls, looking for people to shoot—like it had been a computer game. How had he reduced everything to that? He stared into Turner's eyes again.

"Yeah, you and me," said Coby, his chest aching at the realization. "We killed six people, remember?" And how many had they killed here? Would it all go on forever?

Turner grinned. "Well, now, it's only me, Coby."

The barrel of Turner's rifle leveled at Coby and he fired, the blast exploding into Coby's chest. Coby slammed against the pavement. Above him, the fan was spinning up, the blades obscuring the statue of the girl cradling her foal. Animating her for a brief moment and then blurring her into a bronze haze.

His breathing turned shallow as the dark sky lightened. It wasn't a game. At last, he'd finally gotten it.

THE ESSENCE OF PLACE

Wind swirled dust, silence, and the ages around the survey ship, Iliad. Field archaeologist Hannah Alvarez was the first person out of the ship. With field pack on her shoulder, she stepped onto the ramp, facemask dangling against her blue hazard suit. She hurried to the ramp's end. Scans had indicated the air was breathable. It smelled gritty and dry, but breathable. Hannah studied the horizon with its amber shades of desert and mountains—distant remnants of towers crumbling in the shadows. Gingerly, she stepped onto the sandy soil brushing the edge of the ramp. Hers were the first human footprints to have ever imprinted this alien soil and most likely, the first living soul to stand planetside in centuries. She held her breath, savoring this moment. Nakin'sii—the city of dreams.

Thin, gray shadows lay stark against scraggles of petrified trees and brush interspersed with mounds of sand. Could be burial mounds of some sort. She let out her breath in a soft huff. This world had no known records. Only shadowy references on ancient star charts and remembrances in several alien mythologies. No hint of its streets of gold and sparkling oceans. It was said that alien gods once walked this world, creating their cities and oceans by thought or touch. Ancient travelers had witnessed these moments of creation and described a beauty that the universe had never seen before or since.

"I'm here, Andy," she whispered. "Like we always dreamed. Wish you could have been, too."

She felt so small and insignificant on these vast sandy plains and amid the stillness. Beneath these tiers of sand and centuries lay the legend. Hannah's obsession was to unearth it.

In a few moments, Scott Yoder shuffled down the ramp, a field pack on his left shoulder. Like her, he was a veteran field archaeologist. Scott paused beside her, grinning as he shifted from one side of the ramp to the other, taking in the view. Every step was a bounce, every expression a wide-toothed grin.

"I've looked forward to this fieldwalk for years," he said, his words fast and intense. He motioned at the vestige of a tower that shadowed several sand mounds to the west. "Come with me, Hannah! Let the others unload the gear. This is finally our show."

Scott and Hannah were jointly in charge of this dig, funded by the Lunar Archaeological Institute. She and Scott had earned the privilege by discovering Nakin'sii's location via star charts and years of research. They made a good team. They had been friends since college and had worked together on many deep space excavations. He respected her work and her privacy, never asking questions about Andy's illness and finally his passing, never pressing for details unless she offered them. He'd let her hold onto all the painful particulars without pressure. Scott was her best friend and right now, she needed that.

From the myriad surface scans, they'd chosen this landing site because of its proximity to the ruins and sand mounds. So far, it had been a good choice.

"Fieldwalks come later, Scott," said Hannah in a matter-of-fact voice, holding in her excitement. She didn't want to lose her head. There was too much at stake here. "First, we've got terrain to map out, scan data to compare, success probabilities to run—"

"Come with me," he urged, tugging gently on her arm, a brightness in his eyes.

With his relaxed demeanor, tanned face, and wind-blown hair, he looked like a student on his first summer dig. She admired that. No, she missed it. Her load hadn't been that light in many years. Until now, she'd forgotten how that felt.

"Let go of your archaeologist's training for just a little while,

145

Hannah. We did the work. That's why we're here." He held out his arms and turned in a circle. "Look around you—we're standing in the middle of a legend! Streets of gold . . . prismatic lakes! No human being has ever stepped foot here. Ever! Think about that."

His words carried on the wind, echoing against the arched stone formations scattered across the sea of desert. A chill slipped down Hannah's spine. Machu Picchu, the Martian rock drawings, the Altisan ruins—and now Nakin'sii. She'd dreamed of this moment for nearly twelve years, but it would take a lot of imagination to see those golden streets and rainbowed lakes now. She smiled, studying Scott's intense gaze and anxious pacing. His enthusiasm was always hard to ignore, but on this lost world, it was compelling.

He pointed at the distant sand mounds to the north. Those mounds most likely concealed artifacts no one had ever seen before. But—this dig had to be done right. Procedures followed. Landmarks catalogued and artifacts carefully packed. Otherwise, they might lose things—or cause injuries. She wanted this expedition to be perfect.

"But the sites have to be chosen before nightfall," Hannah insisted, knowing how little time they really had. A little over a month.

He moved toward her, his grin unwavering, and took her by the shoulders.

"Hannah." His soft, insistent voice held her attention. "It's okay to let go a little. Where's your sense of wonder? Where's your excitement? This ancient world left no written records. Nothing! Only images carried forward in alien songs and stories. And now we're standing on their doorstep!"

"All right," Hannah said with a laugh, holding up her hands. "For now, we'll look at possible excavation sites while we walk instead of using the computer scans. I think a random site approach will yield the best finds anyway. We can compare our choices with the computer's tonight."

He sighed in mock weariness, but his smile didn't fade. "Don't get too wild on me, Hannah."

As much as she hated to admit it, Scott was right. Sometimes her fear held her to the tried and true. "Okay, point taken."

He took hold of her arm and squeezed. "Ease that grip a little. Everything will be fine." He pointed to her hand. "Still wearing it?"

Her wedding ring. She nodded and ran her finger over the gold band. It had been exactly ten months since Andy had been cremated. And this was her first dig without him. She had marked the day quietly in her cabin aboard the Iliad, but she just couldn't take off Andy's ring. Not yet. She reached into her field pack and removed her grid mapper, clicking it on. She slipped the band around her wrist. The small device would measure distances as she walked.

"Come on, Let's take that walk. We've earned it," she said and hurried away from the ramp.

They walked west. The planet's silence was overwhelming, only the whisper of their boots and the hollow drone of wind. To think this place had once been a lush, tropical world filled with alien treasures. As she looked out across the vast, haunting stillness, she was overcome by its emptiness. Except for their tiny stream of footprints, the sand lay undisturbed as it had for centuries. She thought of earth and the dead worlds that surrounded it. Would Earth be like this world someday? Could there ever be a time when the oceans dried up and the people turned to dust?

Ahead, in the glare of sunlight, stood the rim of a small crater. She and Scott moved through the rich pool of shadows on the crater's far side.

"Looks too small to be a meteorite impact," Scott muttered, mostly to himself.

"War?" Hannah asked and bent down to examine the depression more closely. Had the inhabitants been conquered or did they destroy themselves?

Scott climbed down into the crater, analyzing size and depth. "Perhaps," he answered finally.

Sand brushed across her face as she turned out of the wind and glanced at the Iliad. The rest of the team, fifteen in all, had already begun unloading the equipment—some on fieldwalks of their own. Edie Masters, pilot and field archaeologist, had struck out on her own walk, leaving a stream of boot prints sizzling in the heat behind her. Her grid mapper flashed red with every step. Good, Hannah wanted the entire team's input. Tonight, after they produced the terrain matrix, she and Scott would listen to the team's suggestions and decide on two excavation sites.

Hannah turned her gaze toward the sand mounds ahead, beyond the tallest remnant tower. It was the site that intrigued her most. Would Andy have agreed or would the arch formations have interested him more? She closed her eyes for a moment, imagining his soft dark curls and his Mediterranean good looks. But so much of him had grown fuzzy. His coat on the hook by the back door—gone now. His bright red toothbrush in the bathroom—gone, too. Those cruddy gray running shoes he wouldn't throw away. She couldn't bring herself to throw them away now. Those images had faded a bit, becoming vague memories. His warm presence beside her at night, the blankets kicked off the bed. The warm smell of his after-shave lingering in the bathroom long after his shower.

"I want to start excavating there," she said to Scott. They only had a short time here before their departure window loomed. If they missed it, it would be months before the next one. And by then, they would have starved to death. It was too much fuel cost to carry more than they needed.

"Let's take a look," he said and hurried out of the crater.

They moved across the rocky terrain toward the lone tower.

"Hey, do you feel that?" Scott asked.

Hannah frowned. "Feel what?"

"Vibrations. They seem to be stronger around the sand mounds."

A soft tremble quivered beneath her dusty brown terrain boots. She stepped closer to the formations and felt the vibrations deepen.

"Do you feel that?"

She nodded. "Yes, of course, but what is it? Seismic activity?"

Scott shook his head. "Doesn't feel like a tremor. It's too steady—too regular."

"Must be some sort of geological phenomenon," she said. The vibrations seemed to deepen as she passed a petrified tree trunk.

Andy would have known. Certified in geochemistry and archaeology, he had lived for moments like this one.

Scott hurried toward the sand mounds, his field kit a dark shadow against his blue hazard suit.

"Wait for me, Scott!" she shouted and her pace quickened.

She caught up to him as he circled the nearest mound. Gently, with his hand, he swept away sand until a patch of pocked, yellow-white stone appeared beneath it.

"Help me clear some of this sand," he muttered.

Reaching into her field pack, Hannah retrieved a small, soft-bristled brush and began to dust away the layers of sand. Anything for a cursory look. Scott followed her lead and pulled his own brush from his field pack. They worked for some time, brushing and smoothing, until the top of a squared column, lying on its side, took shape from within the sand. The elaborate lines scored into the column's capital, twisting and turning, tangled into a beautiful, multidimensional pattern that somewhat reminded Hannah of Celtic knotwork, but much more delicate. It wound around the capital in what appeared to be holographic layers. The design seemed to move with their angle of vision.

Across from the column lay another mound of sand about the same height.

"What do you think, a gateway into a city?"

"Possibly. Perhaps it's the remains of a temple? I want to know what lies beneath it."

Hannah brushed away a bit of sand from the other mound, revealing another swath of yellow-white stone. She slid her datapad out of her fieldkit and strapped the small unit to her wrist. It was half the width of her forearm and at times, bulky, but it freed her hands. She called up a terrain map, a grid where they'd walked already set down from the mappers. When she located the sand mounds, she highlighted the spot as a prime excavation site.

"We'll mark this as a high yield site," she said. "I want to get a cursory reading of the stone's composition."

After she'd attached four small sensors to the site monuments and gathered her data, Hannah pointed out a field of rocks and petrified tree trunks on the horizon. "Let's walk toward that rock field and see what else is here."

Nodding, Scott put away his brush and moved toward the rock field. Hannah fumbled with her own brush as she followed his quick pace. She left the site sensors in place to mark the excavation site.

The air cooled as they approached the rock field. Boulders lay scattered across the fine sheen of ivory sand, stone tree trunks protruding from the landscape. Again, Hannah felt the vibrations. A gentle shaking that trembled up through her boots and into her legs and stomach. It deepened as she moved toward the tree trunk. She laid her hand against the trunk. It felt cool to her touch. How it remained cool in this heat was a mystery, but the air was cooler in this location.

For an instant, images surged forward, overwhelming her. The wedding, the honeymoon on Europa, of returning to a new life on the lunar colony. The smell of sugary icing and burning candles. She felt the rich satin of her wedding dress and the dewy softness of the lilies in her bouquet. The string quartet lamenting a sonata rang in her ears. Andy had swept her off her feet with hand-written sonnets and moonlit strolls. All of it, she could feel all of it!

God, she'd been happy then. She closed her eyes, the images cycling again and again. How comforting they felt—how clear they seemed. Her eyes stung. Andy would wear away with the years, bits and pieces of what he left behind would fade as if he had never existed. Like his clothes she'd finally given away, the house she'd left behind . . . the life they lived was gone without a trace now. Now, no matter how hard she fought it, the memories were growing fuzzy. The sharpness had faded so quickly. Until now.

"Hannah!"

Scott pulled at her arm and her eyes snapped open.

"What's the matter? What's happened?"

His face was pale, his dark eyes wide with concern. "You collapsed against the tree. Is the heat getting to you?"

He steered her away from the tree trunk. She sat down on a mound of sand and he knelt beside her, pressing a bottle of water into her hands.

"No, I'm not hot," she said, the dreamy state slowly dissipating and with it, the clarity and the feeling. She felt numb again. "Would you attach the site sensors?"

Nodding, he opened his pack and retrieved a handful of the round, red sensor discs. He attached them to several of the petrified trunks. She tapped out commands on her datapad and began the data capture sequence. The red transmission light winked on, the data retrieval beginning.

She gazed at the petrified tree trunk she had just touched. The color had darkened to a deep gray, a hint of brown in it. "Something's odd here."

Hannah rose from the sand and moved toward the tree trunk. She dropped to her knees and pressed her hand against it, examining its pocked surface.

Andy's angry words stung her ears. "I don't know what's happened to you, Hannah. Sometimes, you're as cold as the artifacts we bring home. It's like you leave little parts of yourself out there with every dig." His words lingered, lying heavy against her chest, the strong scent of cedar and vanilla overwhelming—Andy's cologne. She gasped for a breath and stumbled backward. It was all too real. Too intense.

"Talk to me, Hannah," said Scott, a frightened look in his eyes.

"Let's go back to the ship," she said in a hurried tone and turned away. "I want to analyze some of this data before tonight."

Retracing her steps, she moved toward the Iliad. Scott tried to talk to her about what had happened, but she side-stepped his questions.

That evening, after the others had returned to the ship, Hannah assembled everyone's data and site choices. She still had a few milestones left on her physical chemistry certification, but Andy had always filled in the gaps. From the ship's portal, she watched the others sitting on the ramp pointing out landmarks on the darkening horizon. Their lanterns grew brighter as the night settled around them, thick and silent. Their chatter was bright against the dull whirs of the computer crunching data.

On the shelf by the door stood Andy's urn. She'd chosen an artifact from their first deep space dig. A simple Altisan urn glazed in rich teal. She sighed. Andy would have liked that.

She leaned back in her chair, the room smelling of recycled air and stale tea, and studied the printouts. Her Darjeeling had grown ice cold. Many of the proposed sites contained nothing out of the ordinary—until she examined the data collected from the sites west of the Iliad. Several things stood out and she sat up.

Many of the stone formations and the petrified tree trunks contained components unknown to the computer, but all of them had one similarity. All of them contained carbon-silicon-based structures. Her mouth fell open. Some sort of unknown linking element was present in the hybrid structures, allowing them to cross handedness between elements and create molecular chains. Somehow, the structures had broken down silica into easily excreted wastes. If this was true, then these formations could have once been organic life forms.

She had chosen the site of the first dig.

Hannah rose from her desk. She paused at Andy's urn and ran her fingers across it, wishing she could share her discovery with him. She would never stop missing him. Turning away, she carried the data out of her cramped compartment. She hurried down the narrow hallway to the ramp. The crew's voices were louder now. She stepped through the open airlock and out into the cool night air. The thin, ruddy glow of the lanterns made their excited faces look wild.

"Everyone, I've chosen the first site," she said. "Scott will choose the second one."

Conversations halted. "Where?" someone cried.

Hannah pointed to the west. "The stone formations."

"What about the ocean bed?" Edie asked, disappointment evident in her thin face.

"Don't worry, Edie, it's under consideration as the second site. But the tower and stone formations have yielded some—interesting results. The chemical analysis shows the presence of organic compounds—carbon-based and," Hannah paused, unable to hold back her smile. "Silicon-based."

"Impossible!" Scott shouted.

She turned to Scott. "That's what I thought, too, but there is some sort of unknown linking element . . . it's incredible! The stone may have once been some sort of living entity."

"We have just over four weeks to excavate before the launch window arrives, so we have to work quickly," said Scott.

Excitement buzzed through the silence now as the other archaeologists gathered around her, anxious to view the data. She handed out the sheets and a complete matrix of the excavation site. Edie held one of the lanterns over the printout as Scott and the others studied the analysis.

While they pondered the numbers, Hannah sat down on the ramp, her legs dangling, and breathed in the dry night air of Nakin'sii. She gazed at the darkening horizon with reverence. What dreams lay beneath Nakin-sii's hard-packed soil? At last, Hannah would know.

The next morning, at first light, the entire crew headed to the stone formations. Edie oversaw the small robotic trench cutter and sifter. The rest of the crew watched, shovels in hand, as the first trench was slowly carved into the hard, dry soil. The trench cutter's echolocation sensors would prevent it from destroying all but the tiniest find.

Slowly and painstakingly, the dig took shape. Sehamba, an associate professor from Niger, served as draughtsperson, generating computer drawings of the first trench. Scott handled the stratigraphic equipment, analyzing soil layers and producing context information for each layer. Hannah and the rest of the team had run string to produce the grid lines that Edie used to guide the digging.

Hannah wandered to the edge of the site, her gaze turning westward. She thought of Andy and the odd experience she'd had in the rock field. Until the trench-cutter was finished, she wouldn't be missed. Quietly, she wandered away from the site, moving across the pristine sand, yesterday's footprints guiding her.

When she reached the field, the petrified trunk she'd touched stood out from the others. Glossy white bark covered the trunk and pale gray/green shoots had sprouted from the dead limb stumps. And in the sand . . . she fell to her knees to examine it. Everywhere she and Scott had stood were footprint-shaped patches of pale mauve and green grass. Nakin'sii was coming to life!

She turned and ran across the sand, back the way she'd come. As soon as she neared the site, she shouted for Scott. He rushed out to meet her.

"Hannah? What's wrong?"

"It's incredible! Come look!"

His face was a mask of worry, no doubt afraid something terrible had happened.

"What's happened?"

"Something wonderful," she said in a soft voice.

Work halted at the site as the others followed Hannah out to the rock field.

Scott gasped. "The trees—they're growing! But they were petrified?"

All throughout the field, tiny white patches of bark glittered in the sunlight. Mauve-green grasses had pushed through the sand all over the rock field.

Hannah ran through the field, past other dormant trunks until she'd reached the far end. She had to know if the phenomenon occurred throughout the tree trunks. She knelt and pressed her hand against the trunk, thinking of her favorite times with Andy. A chill shivered through her spine and softly Andy's voice whispered in her ear. She felt his hands against her arms, his lips brushing her cheek. His presence, she felt his presence beside her.

"Andy?" she called, her eyes snapping open.

She slid back, looking frantically for him, almost expecting to see him leaning against the tree trunk, arms crossed and grinning mischievously. There had been such fire in his soul and she missed it desperately. Her eyes burned and she bit her lip.

Slowly, she stood. The bark on the dormant, stone tree was returning, grass sprouting all around it. Hannah moved through the rock field, watching the others examining the trunks and reexperiencing their most treasured memories. It was the city of dreams, sharpening what time had blunted. It was as if the stone synthesized nerve impulses that made up memories and emotions and replayed them. No—initiated them. These things weren't petrified trees. The stone was some sort of living entity that needed human contact to bring it out of this strange state of hibernation.

Standing on the periphery of the rock field, she was soon joined by Scott. The others trickled out of the field, strangely silent. In their faces, she saw that they had been through intensely private emotions and memories. Beyond the field, the stone formations silently marked their excavation site. Grass had sprouted in the footprints leading across the sand toward the site. The city of dreams was waking.

When they returned to the dig site, the trench had been filled in, no signs of the trench cutter's movements visible in the sand. All the strings had snapped and lay in coils on the sand. And slowly those coils were being transformed into green vines. The fallen, broken capitals were taking on a pearlescent sheen and the cracks had filled in, broken sections restored.

"What's happening?" Edie replied as she hurried toward the idle robots. "The trench has been filled in and they've shut down."

"It's Nakin'sii," was all Hannah could say.

Over the next four weeks, Hannah and her crew watched Nakin'sii rebuild itself, producing familiar trees and plants alongside species they'd never seen before. The grass had burned across the sand, igniting it into flames of mauve-green grass that spread over the horizon in all directions. In the distance, pearly structures rose, capitals standing tall and straight, roofs capping broken walls, and streets! Smooth, golden ribbons rose from the sands, stretching across the newly formed grasslands. Streets of gold. Soon, though, they'd have to leave this place. The launch window was only days away.

Hannah stood at the end of the Iliad's ramp, cradling her field pack against her side. There was something she had to do before the launch window arrived. She started across the grassland, toward the forest that had once been the rock field.

"Hannah!" Edie shouted, running toward her from the north. "Come see!"

"What did you find?" Hannah called.

Edie reached her at last and chest heaving, she bent to catch her breath. In a few moments, she could speak.

"Do you hear it?" she asked finally.

Hannah frowned. "Hear what?"

"Listen," said Edie, grinning.

Hannah fell silent, listening to the wind. She shook her head, still frowning, but then she heard the gentle whisper. Of ocean waves.

"The dried up ocean bed!" she cried.

Edie nodded. "I heard it early this morning. And there are dolphins, Hannah! Dolphins! Let me show you."

Hannah laid her hand to her field pack. "In a little while," she answered. "There's something I've got to do first."

A puzzled look touched Edie's face. She brushed a brown wisp of hair out of her eyes and nodded. "Sure. Walk north from the Iliad and you can't miss it." The smile returned to her face. "I mean, it's an ocean—how can you miss it."

"Okay," Hannah said with a laugh. "I'll be there soon." She turned away and walked toward the forest of white-barked trees, holding her field pack very carefully.

The air smelled warm and faintly of flower essences—even the tang of sea salt. She felt the air cool slightly as she entered the lush woods that slowly expanded across the sand. When she was certain none of the crew was around, she set down her field pack.

From it, she removed Andy's urn. She reached out to the nearest tree and ran her fingers along the bark. Her memories sparked, clear and intense. Here, Andy would never fade.

Opening the urn, she scattered his ashes around the base of the tree.

Everywhere the ashes fell, small, yellow and red flowers pushed through the soil and blossomed. The dewy petals shimmered, looking like flames. The flowers' heady scent smelled of cedar and vanilla—Andy's cologne. Tears welled in her eyes as the air grew warm and she felt his touch against her face. She cupped the air, hearing him whisper her name.

When Hannah found her way to the ocean, she stood on the ridge, stunned by the massive expanse. The surge and ebb of the waves filled her with peace. The ocean had a pale crystal sheen of lightest amethyst to it. And the dolphins, four of them, leaped and spun just off shore. Scott sat in the sand while six other team members walked the beach. Edie waded out toward the dolphins and they swam playfully around her tall, thin frame.

Scott motioned Hannah over and she sat down beside him.

"I can't believe what we found here," he said. "Part is our memories and part is from somewhere else. And in three days, our launch window will be here."

She nodded. That realization had nagged at her for some time. She watched her pilot communing with dolphins, most likely the first time in her life. Edie didn't seem any more ready to leave this place than the others.

"To think all of this lay dormant," said Hannah. "No wonder Nakin'sii has been lost all this time. It took a lot of imagination to believe this was the right place."

"I've had Sehamba recording as many images of Nakin'sii as we can store," said Scott. "I've been collecting samples of the vegetation, fresh water, salt water, everything I can catalog."

Scott continued to explain his data collection, but Hannah's attention wandered to Edie and the dolphins. The only way to study this world was to be here. But taking samples back was only a piece of its essence. It wasn't enough to gain an understanding. She wasn't sure if Scott had finished talking when she rose from the sand and walked into the surf to join Edie and the dolphins.

The remaining three days passed like seconds until inevitably, the launch window was upon them. Scott had overseen the departure preparations and Hannah was grateful for that. Everyone filed out of the Iliad to take one last fieldwalk of Nakin'sii. Hannah carried her field pack, all of her necessary possessions inside it. She wasn't going back. She was a field archaeologist and used to performing post mortems on cultures, not making first contact. She couldn't go back to doing post mortems. Not after Nakin'sii.

She followed the others in their solemn last walk to the Iliad, but stopped at the end of the ramp. Scott was halfway up the ramp when he realized she wasn't behind him.

"What is it, Hannah?"

"I'm not going back with you. I'm staying behind to study this world."

His mouth gaped. "Stay behind? Hannah, you can't! Who knows when anyone else will return here?" He took two steps toward her, but something in her expression made him stop. "Hannah—you can't," he said in a quiet voice. "You'll be all alone here."

The rest of the team huddled in the doorway of the Iliad. Then Edie pushed through, field pack on her shoulder.

"No, she won't. I'm staying, too. This place is a researcher's dream. Jorge is my backup. He can take the Iliad home."

One by one, the other team members left the Iliad, lingering on the ramp. Sehamba touched Scott's shoulder, a smile on her dark face. "It's too important to leave behind," she said, her tone respectful as she slipped past him.

He stood there alone on the ramp. Hannah moved toward him. "Before we came here, Nakin'sii was only a reference. Only through us has the city become the legend we sought. If we leave, it will return to the dust. If we stay, it will survive."

For a long while, Scott was silent. Finally, he nodded. "You're right. I'll send a transmission to the Institute, letting them know we are staying indefinitely." The weight seemed to lift from Scott's shoulders. Relief shined in his eyes as his gaze met Hannah's. He didn't want to leave either, she realized.

"I'll meet you on the shore," she said.

Hannah moved toward the gold ribbon that led north. The air smelled of cedar and vanilla, her memories sharp and focused, as she walked a newly created street in the city of dreams.

MUSIC TO HER EARS

"Sleep well, Miss Eleanor," said the weary-eyed orderly. He reached for the velcro bed straps. "Your daughter and her husband will be in early. They've got something to discuss with you."

Eleanor Canada Newell, paper-white skin clinging to her furrowed face and puckered lips, shook her head at the straps, her delft blue eyes desperate. She gazed from the straps to the music box on the nightstand.

The orderly sighed and crossed his arms. "This is for your own good, Miss Eleanor. I don't want to come in here and find you lying in the floor again. Last time, it took four weeks for those fractures to heal."

"Please, Harvey. Let me sleep in peace tonight," she said, a whisper of the South in her voice. "Just for tonight." She already knew what news her daughter, Brenda, brought.

Harvey talked strict, but he'd been sweet to her since she'd arrived here, sneaking her butter cookies and hot tea in the evenings. He gazed down at the over-starched sheets. "All right," he said, wagging a finger at her. "But just for tonight."

He opened the door, the scalding hallway lights cutting through the cool darkness of her room, but she called gently to him.

"Harvey, could you wind my music box before you go?"

She pointed a skeletal finger toward the rosewood and glass music box on the nightstand.

He paused in the threshold, silhouetted by the harsh light, and glanced back at her. "Can't you go one night without playing that box? You've played it every night since you been here."

Three months she'd been here—after a fall in her kitchen. They told her she could go home as soon as she had healed. He didn't know how much that music box meant to her, especially now.

When she didn't answer, he groaned and ran his hand across his spiky blond bangs. Finally, he reached for the music box.

"Thank you."

"Don't know what's so special about this thing."

"My husband, God rest his soul, won it for me on prom night, the night he proposed."

He smiled. "Good night, Miss Eleanor. Tomorrow's going to be a busy day."

The music box's crisp chime plinked out *In the Good Ol' Summer Time* as Harvey slipped out of the room. Eleanor closed her eyes, savoring the timeworn melody. The cool darkness and the notes intertwined with her breathing until the veils of her memory parted.

The clop of horse and carriage replaced the clinking of dishes from the hallway. The starched sheet became a white pinafore draping her frame. Slowly, she swung her fragile body off the bed, her feet touching the cold, dusty linoleum. With unsteady limbs, she reached for the music box. It vibrated in her hands as she carried it toward the closed door. Fighting against her aching body, she bent down and set the music box in front of the door.

She reached beneath the lid and plucked a tarnished corsage pin from the pink velvet interior. She smiled. From her prom corsage. The faux pearl on top of the pin had yellowed, but it was still ramrod straight. She attached it to the lace collar of her nightgown.

The song's summery chorus filled her soul until the bricks of Seaside's misty Promenade hardened beneath her feet. The turn-of-the-century sparkled in the music box's beveled glass top and she reached her quivering hands through the glass toward it.

The weight of the decades stripped away from her until the salt-tanged air was cool against her smooth, taut skin. Pain left her spine and knees. She reached back, grateful to find her thick braid of sable hair pinned beneath her white hat. The corsage pin glowed with a white-gold sheen. The rush of waves mixed with the sounds of the music box.

A few hundred feet down the Promenade, lamplighters lit gas lamps. One by one, the lamps winked on in the misty twilight. Girls in white prom dresses adorned with pastel ribbons strolled past, smiling gentlemen with slicked back hair and white coats on their arms. Colored parasols to ward off the sea mist sprouted up and down the Promenade, shielding wide-brimmed, floral hats tied with scarves over Gibson Girl hair. The twitter of voices echoed down the walkway. She smiled. Prom night 1916.

From the dance hall terrace, violins lamented a waltz haunted by the soft echo of piano. Shadows danced in the gas-lit twilight. The prom was in full swing.

There on the turnaround stood a man in a pressed white coat and a boater hat. He leaned against one of the walkway posts, the flicker of lamplight across his face. He smiled at her and tipped his hat, hiding his sandy-colored hair.

"Miss Eleanor," he cooed.

"Arthur Newell," she said, the South stronger in her voice now. "Have you been waiting long?"

"Not long," he said, his face handsome and freshly shaven. He smiled and his brown eyes warmed her.

She sat down on a wooden bench. He followed, sitting beside her. Seagulls fluttered nearby and she watched them land on the Promenade, pecking at flecks of peanut shells and sugarplums scattered around a trash receptacle. Behind her, Shaker chimes from the prom night carnival brightened the maudlin waltz, drowning out the music box that still echoed in her ears. Laughter and bells punctuated the rush of the sea. She even remembered the prom's theme now: Summer Magic. Beyond the terrace, there were tea cookies and cakes, old friends, and carnival games.

"Do you want to play some of the carnival games tonight?" Arthur asked. "Or how about a carriage ride down the coast?" He glanced at a young couple who sat down on a bench across the turnaround. The girl twirled her pink parasol and giggled, covering her mouth with a white-gloved hand. Pink roses wrapped around her wrist.

"One night is never enough time, is it?"

"No, Arthur," Eleanor answered and reached for his hands. She held them against her lips and kissed them. "Tonight, will you just hold me and tell me you love me?"

He laughed, the sound of summer and daisies in his voice. "Silly girl, I always tell you that just before I propose to you. Remember?"

He put his arms around her waist, rustling her pinafore and she snuggled closer to him. Like the flow and ebb of an ocean wave, the Shaker chimes crescendoed and fell silent.

"I thought you might be tired of it and would want something else tonight," Arthur said with a sigh. "You've heard me say I love you every night for three months now."

"And I never tire of it, love," she answered, closing her eyes.

He leaned over and pinned a gardenia corsage to her dress just as he had done that prom night in 1916. The sweet smell of his bay rum and the heady scent of gardenias made her feel eighteen and giddy again. Like the sugary taste of tea cookies at her first high tea. Or the spring social where she wore her first pair of silk, elbow-length gloves. Or the glitter of an engagement ring on her finger. She opened her eyes when she felt Arthur slide the ring onto her finger.

The marquis diamond made her cheeks burn with delight. She held her hand out until the flicker of gas lamps caught the ring. Finally, she leaned over and kissed Arthur on the lips. He pulled her closer.

"I wasn't sure if you were tired of the ring. I tried to make it different this time, but that carnival fortune teller told me that part was etched into the chimes. No way to change it."

She pulled back from him. "Don't change a thing, Arthur. I want everything as it was on prom night, the night you won the music box. Remember?"

He took off his boater hat and scratched his head. "My memory's not so good anymore, Ellie."

"I'm not surprised, love," she said, "considering you passed on three months ago. I feel badly that I keep calling you back to me like this, but the nursing home is so lonely. Besides, I miss you terribly."

He took her into his arms again and she reached up, running her fingers across his smooth jaw line. The white daisy in his lapel felt dewy against her fingers.

"I missed you, too. I didn't know you'd even kept that old box until I smelled the salt air and the peanuts roasting. When I saw the gas lamps guttering, I knew you'd kept it—that the old Gypsy had been telling the truth."

She pulled him up from the bench and hooked her arm in his. "Walk with me, Arthur. Walk through 1916 again with me."

He plucked the daisy from his lapel and handed it to her, bowing. She smiled and pressed it to her nose, knowing daisies had no scent, but it smelled of 1916. Everything smelled of horse-drawn carriages, sugarplums, and fresh lemonade. Of pinafores, pin-striped suits, and boater hats. For a few more hours, it would all smell of 1916 until sunrise brought back the smell of moth balls, oatmeal, and bleach mixed with urine.

"I have a surprise for you," said Eleanor. She dashed down the Promenade, pausing underneath a gas lamp. The cool sea mist caressed her face and she wanted to shake her long hair loose.

He chased after her, laughing. Taking hold of the lamp pole, he whirled around and around it, always pausing to gaze at her as he moved past. She watched him turn in time with the waltz music, tracing the age lines that would appear on his youthful face with the years. The bullet wound in his left leg from World War I, the scar across his hand from breaking the window in their first house. The curve of his spine from years at a desk job he despised. There was no sign yet of the boredom that set in after his retirement, no sign of the cancer that would kill him. The flame that had first drawn her burned hot and alive in him tonight, like the dancing flames of the gas lamps.

"What is it, Ellie?"

"I was just remembering," she said, her Southern accent growing wistful as the sea mist thickened. "I think I've fixed it so we can stay here forever."

His eyes widened. He stopped turning and moved toward her, taking her by the shoulders. "How?"

"Remember how that gypsy told us to be careful with the music box. Even a crack or a bent pin could ruin the magic."

He nodded. "She said if you or I broke it, we could never come back."

"What if someone else breaks it? While we're here?"

"I don't know, Ellie? We never asked her that. What are you saying?"

She smiled. "I've fixed it so it will break before dawn. Harvey does his rounds about 5 am. When he opens the door, he'll hit the music box. When it breaks, we'll be together—here—forever."

His expression turned sad, almost frightened. "What if you're sent back and can never return and I'm stuck here forever—without you."

She gasped and grabbed his arms. "I don't know." She hadn't even considered that possibility. "Back there, I was so sure it would work, but now, looking into your eyes, I wish I hadn't. I'd rather spend the nights I have left with you than without you."

From the dance hall terrace, the Shaker chimes sent their tinny chords across the Promenade, the violin's sad notes trembling above them. It sounded like a pipe organ, the merry strains comforting. There, at that prom night carnival, she and Arthur had won the music box with its magical tune, just as the fortune teller had promised. Eleanor had kept it safe in her hope chest for when she or Arthur would need it. Arthur's frightened gaze unnerved her and she couldn't look away, afraid that if she blinked he would dissolve in front her like cotton candy in rain.

"Let's talk to the Gypsy woman," she said. "She can tell us what will happen before sunrise."

"What good will that do now?"

"Come on," she said, tugging on his sleeve. "Let's find the fortune teller. We should be at the carnival anyway."

Nodding reluctantly, he took her hand and she pulled him toward the prom night carnival.

Firecrackers and sparklers crackled like popping corn through the Seaside street as carnival performers in their brilliant silks juggled brightly colored balls. Some did hand stands and back flips, others coaxed terriers to jump through hoops. Carnival games lined the street that led toward the beach. A couple rushed by, pink taffy stringing from their hands. Other couples lingered in front of the game booths, gazing at the prizes. Down at the end of the booths, farthest from the Promenade, stood Madame Ralenka's fortune telling tent. A heavy swath of amethyst velvet covered the entrance and a man in a skimmer hat stood in front. His over waxed moustache matched the slickness of his dark hair. He pointed his cane at Arthur's chest and smiled wryly.

"How'd you like to see your destiny, young man?" He waved the cane through the air. "Madame Ralenka knows all. Find out the strength of her powers."

Arthur cast a quick glance at Eleanor who nodded slightly. He gave the man a nod. Slowly, the man reached out and lifted the velvet curtain. With reticent steps, Arthur ducked under the velvet, Eleanor behind him.

Inside, a round table draped with ruby and amethyst satin stood in the center of the tent. The air looked as misty as the Promenade except for the crystal ball in the center of the table. The woman, gold charms and bells draped around her wrists and neck, jangled as she motioned toward the crystal ball. Her coarse, ebony hair hung wild around her dark face and made-up eyes.

"Come. Sit with me," she said, her Romanian accent thick. "I show you your destinies."

Eleanor sat down in the chair closest to the crystal ball, just as she had in 1916. The Gypsy woman studied her for a few moments and then stared at Arthur.

"I seen you before, no?"

"Yes," Eleanor answered. "On a long ago prom night like this one, you told us about the music box. Do you remember?"

The woman smiled. "Yes, the box. I tell you if you win it on prom night, you and husband never be apart."

"Yes, but you told us to be very careful," said Arthur, leaning forward.

"Box is very old. From an old Romanian sorceress in the old country. The magic was woven between you when you first won music box. If you or she break box, you never return to the night you win it."

Eleanor gripped the edges of her skirt. "What if someone else breaks the music box, while Arthur and I are here?"

The Gypsy shook her head. "Then magic will be lost."

"Will we be trapped here forever?"

"No. The magic bond between you is fragile. If it break, no one can return here."

"This can't be!" Eleanor shrieked, leaping up from her chair. "Is there anyway to go back before the sun rises?"

"Is not possible. The magic was woven at night, so only works at night." The woman reached out to Eleanor and touched the daisy in her hand. "Is pretty."

"I bought it from a little dark-haired girl selling them on the Promenade, before you arrived, Ellie."

"A fragile thing, like the box," said the Gypsy. "My daughter sells these by the sea. You pin on to be safe. That is all I can say."

Slowly, Eleanor rose from the chair and holding onto Arthur, she walked out into the night.

Eleanor sat on a bench in Arthur's arms and cried into her handkerchief as she waited for the sun to rise. The music had faded from the terrace along with the Shaker chimes. Slowly, the horizon lightened to gray and then the lamplighters arrived to turn out the lamps. She could hear the whir and snap as the lamps, one by one, were snuffed out.

"I don't want to say goodbye, Arthur," said Eleanor in a tear-strained voice. "I want to be with you forever."

He held her tighter, resting his chin against her cheek. "And I you, Ellie." He sat up and made her look at him. "We had each other three months longer than most people got."

The tears rushed down her cheeks. "But it isn't enough. Especially now. I can't leave you like this!"

"I loved you, Eleanor," he said, making her look at him.

"Remember that. Especially the woman who stayed at my bedside and held my hand as my life slipped from this world. That woman, I love as much, maybe more than fiery, 18-year-old Eleanor Canada who captured my heart back in 1916."

An off-key chord chimed through the silent town of Seaside and Eleanor shivered, the wind coming off the ocean suddenly cold.

"Arthur Newell, I fell in love with you the day I met you and even when I lost you, I never stopped loving you. You will be with me always. Hold my hand now."

Arthur rose from the bench and held out his hand. "Dance with me, Eleanor."

Nodding, Eleanor stood. Arthur slid an arm around her waist and gripped her right hand in his. Dancing to the sound of the waves and the dowsing of the gas lamps, Eleanor and Arthur waltzed down the Promenade.

Glass shattered. Arthur held her hand tighter and she gripped his as the sea mist settled thick on the Promenade, obscuring the gas lamps and benches. Arthur's steps quickened and they twirled faster. Wood splintered. Eleanor laid her head against Arthur's shoulder and wept.

Seaside disappeared in the mist, Arthur, prom night, and the Promenade fading into the predawn grayness as the veil of Eleanor's memory fell over 1916. It was then that she felt him let go of her hands.

Eleanor awoke to Harvey's rough hands placing her back in her bed. Bits of wood and glass littered the floor, a custodian sweeping them into a metal dust pan. Tears funneled down her wrinkled face and plopped onto stiff white sheets.

"Miss Eleanor, you gave me quite a scare!" cried Harvey, out of breath. "I'm sorry about your music box. I didn't see it by the door."

She wanted to apologize, but couldn't find the words. Arthur was gone and so was the music box. Her selfishness had taken it all away. She reached up to wipe away her tears and felt a softness against her face. Pulling her hand away, she saw Arthur's daisy peeking through her fingers. She kissed the flower and cradled it against her cheek.

"Are you in pain anywhere?"

Her chest ached, but she shook her head.

"Mom?" Brenda called from the doorway. She stepped over to the bed. "What's the matter? Are you all right?"

Harvey smiled at her as he moved toward the door. "She fell out of bed again, but it looks like she was lucky this time. No breaks or fractures. We'll get her down to the doctor this afternoon though, just to be safe." Harvey hurried into the hallway, leaving Eleanor alone with her daughter and son-in-law.

"Good morning, honey," said Eleanor. "How are you?"

Brenda, looking much older than Eleanor remembered, leaned down and kissed her on the cheek. Her blonde hair was streaked with gray, the lines thick around her mouth and eyes. She looked frightened. Eleanor looked past Brenda, at her burly, silent husband leaning against the wall. Husband number two. She hoped this would be Brenda's last one, a man who treated her right.

"I'm fine. Now, what's this important news you have for me." Eleanor knew she would never leave this nursing home. She knew what Brenda would tell her.

"Mom, we found a buyer for your house. I need your signature on these papers to sell it. But I need it today." Tears welled in Brenda's eyes. Eleanor reached out to her and Brenda took her hand.

"I didn't want it to be this way, Mom, I didn't! I wanted you to come live with me, but the doctor says that isn't possible now."

Eleanor smiled and patted Brenda's hand. Over the years, arthritis had nearly crippled Eleanor. Her brittle bones could crack by turning over wrong in bed. "It's all right, dear. I knew. It's okay now. Sell the house. Without Arthur, it just wasn't a home anymore."

"But I'll come visit you every day," said Brenda, wiping away her tears. "I promise I will."

"I know you will, honey." Eleanor stroked the daisy with her fingers. Brenda meant well, but she had no understanding of how it felt in here. Poor thing had her own troubles and Eleanor didn't want to add to them.

After Eleanor signed the house papers, she ate her breakfast and listened to Brenda talk about Eleanor's grandchildren. How well they were doing in school. Finally, Brenda rose from the chair and hugged her.

"I'll be back to see you tomorrow night, Mom. I love you."

Eleanor squeezed Brenda's hand. "I love you too, dear."

As soon as the door closed, Eleanor knew she had to try one last time to return to 1916. Fighting down her panic, Eleanor pressed the daisy to her heart and began to hum. A cart squeaked by her door. Someone coughed. Concentrating, she scrunched her eyes closed and hummed louder, but prom night 1916 was beyond her reach.

Sobs trembled through her frail body as she kissed the daisy. The little flower was so fragile. Then she remembered the fortuneteller had said something about the daisy's fragileness. That Eleanor should keep it safe. She smiled. Like she had told her to keep the music box safe all those years ago.

Laying her hand to her lapel, she found the yellowed corsage pin. Gently, she pinned it through the daisy's stem and against her nightgown. She hummed louder. The corsage pin began to gleam. Closing her eyes, Eleanor clutched the daisy.

The veils of her memory parted. Above the Shaker chimes piping *In the Good Ol' Summer Time* across the Promenade, Arthur called her name. Eleanor went to him. Waves whispered against the sand, autumn sharp in the cool air as Arthur took her in his arms. Laughing, he twirled her around and around. Eleanor tossed her hat into the air and at last, she shook her sable braid free. One by one, the gas lamps went dark and as first light touched the Promenade, Eleanor and Arthur danced.

The next morning, Brenda and Harvey found Eleanor cold and gray in the floor beside her bed, a fresh daisy pinned to her nightgown. Harvey comforted Brenda as best he could, telling her that Eleanor hadn't been in pain, that her heart had just given out.

But Eleanor knew otherwise. Her heart hadn't given out. It had given in.

THE SPIRIT HOUSE

Cast your soul to the sea, he said to me once. From some stupid love poem he wrote. Donny always talks weird, in romantic images that are pretty but empty. Like Donny. He's serving ten to life down in Walla Walla. Sometimes I even miss him.

From this pier, if I close my eyes, I can still see him in those heavy boots walking the surf-soaked rocks where we used to sit and talk. He loves to walk the shore. Maybe that's why he says those stupid things? Maybe they somehow make up for the bad things he did—we did. I try to remember that, but sometimes, my head's all confused. It's the new rehab treatment they gave me today.

Carmen Slater, my probation officer, stands at the opposite end of the pier, waiting for me. She doesn't usually follow me around like this, but my community service starts today, so she's sticking close. I glance down at the thick black band around my ankle. This tracking device will lead them right to me if I decide to bolt. Not many places for a convicted felon to run.

Still, I'm lucky. I got out in five with a stint in rehab and community service. It'll be a year before I'm through with both. I didn't kill that guy in the alley that night (Donny did), but I did gank his money. Donny told the guy if he handed over his cash, he wouldn't shoot him. Stupid fool made Donny kill him. Over twenty bucks and a lousy credit card.

"Kip, it's time to go!"

I turn away from the ocean and stare blankly at Carmen with her severe black hair, stuffy lace blouse, and over-pressed blue skirt. Like some store window mannequin. Carmen taps her watch. "I need to get you to the hospice now." Her words are loud and slow. Don't know if she thinks I'm deaf or stupid. She reminds me of my fourth grade teacher, always talking to me like I don't understand English. I hated Mrs. Williams. I don't have much use for Carmen either.

She motions me away from the pier and slowly, I comply. I'll come in my own time. Finally, I reach her and with a smirk, I slip past her into the car. I lean my face against the window to catch another glimpse of the ocean. My hair smells salty and clean from the breeze. Carmen frowns, but she puts on that fake, everything's-okay smile and slides into the driver's seat. Then she drives away, toward some stupid hospice where I'm supposed to do my CS. There's some experiment going on there and I'm part of it. Some choice—the rest of my prison term or some bullshit experiment. I'd rather be picking up trash in parks, but I guess my gig's easier than Donny's. He may never see the ocean again.

Carmen drives out of the parking lot and onto the highway. The Puget Sound flickers at the edges of the rocky, tree-covered shoreline rushing ahead of us. The pines are so tall and green against the bare trees around them. Autumn came fast this year.

My head still hurts from the rehab session. I thought it'd be some sort of therapy where they'd talk at me and give me drugs, but it turned into minor surgery. Some chaff about a device to signal some brain chemicals to be released. The doctor showed it to me. It's smaller than an aspirin. How can something that small do anything? I don't quite understand it all and I don't want this thing in my head, but it beats that rat-trap cell and getting a shiv in the gut some night. They say I don't know right from wrong, but this thing in my head does and eventually, it will teach me. One of the doctors calls it an artificial conscience. Guess if Donny and me had had this thing, he wouldn't have killed that jerk in Seattle. A twinge of pain ripples through my stomach and my hands start to shake, like I'm hungry or something.

"We're not far from the hospice, Kip," Carmen chirps from the front seat, all smiles and bouncy. Like we're going on a picnic. She's so fake she makes me sick. "It's just past Coupeville."

The blue and green water is bright against the steep cliffs that rise around us. I close my eyes, not realizing I've fallen asleep until Carmen gently nudges my shoulder.

"Kip, we're here. Kip?"

I step out of the car and stare at the cedar building on the hillside. With all its windows, it looks fragile, like a strong wind would knock it over. A thin curl of smoke rises into the gray sky. The air smells burnt.

"This is Crossroads Hospice," says Carmen. She carries my duffle bag with her toward the front door and I have no choice but to follow. I hate this thing on my ankle.

A silver-haired woman opens the door and greets Carmen like a long-lost relative. She's short and squat and looks like she should have eleven grandchildren.

"Carmen, how are you? It's been ages, child!" The old woman hugs her.

"How are you, Miss Miller? It's so good to see you again." Carmen grips the old woman's plump arms.

The woman shakes a finger at Carmen. "It's Mary Margaret."

Carmen slips over to me and puts her hands on my shoulders, but I pull away. "Mary Margaret, this is Kelly Thorpe."

I sneer. I haven't been Kelly Thorpe in a long, long time.

"I go by Kip."

The old woman's expression turns serious as she stares at me, looking through me. Uncomfortable, I look away. "You've got quite a bit of work ahead of you, Kelly Thorpe." She pauses and the hint of a smile touches her wrinkled, pale face. "Kip."

I shrug. So, I empty a few bedpans and change a few sheets. Big deal. Doesn't mean anything. In a year, I'll be out of here. I'll head south, toward San Diego. That'll be far enough from this state.

My stomach hurts again, but I keep a straight face.

Old Mary Margaret opens the door and waves me inside. I glare at her as I pick up my bag and walk past. She's gotta get the message right off that I'm not interested in being her friend. I'm just here to do my time. I'll be their little maze jockey as long as I get my chocolate bar.

The inside of this place looks like something out of those old, liver-colored photographs, where the clothes were bulky and fussy, full of lace and velvet and frills. Lots of fancy curtains and table coverings. Flowers everywhere. And it stinks of roses. I remember Donny taking me to a flower shop once. The case was full of roses, all kinds of colors, all kinds of smells. But this place reeks of them. Glass lamps sit in front of the windows and reflect light in little rainbows around the one big room. There are couches everywhere and eight or nine people sitting there in robes. Most of them stare blankly around the room through sunken eyes and hollowed faces. I smile. Like those store window dummies. Better them than me.

Old Mary Margaret's face tightens when she sees my smile.

"Is there something you find amusing here, Kip?"

"This place looks more like a wax museum than a nursing home," I answer. Again, my stomach burns, the pain a little worse than before. I must be coming down with something.

Mary Margaret glares at me and points to the hallway. Smirking, I move toward it.

She walks ahead, past what looks like a dining room and kitchen. At the end of the hall is a large bunk room. There's thick pink and blue comforters on each bed. A blonde woman in blue scrubs walks through the room, adjusting covers, filling water pitchers that set on little, marble-top tables beside the beds. Most of the beds are filled with thin people, like they're going to kick off any minute.

"This where you keep the stiffs?" I ask.

Mary Margaret turns and grabs me by the shoulders. She shakes me hard, like I'd just spit on her shoes or something. Her face is all red and her lips are pressed together. I shove her away.

"Don't do that again," I say. I don't like people touching me.

A sharp pain rips through my gut and I cry out, falling to my knees. Her hands grip my shoulders again, but she doesn't shake me this time.

"Kip—"

I slap her hands away. "Leave me alone!"

Again, the pain rips through my gut like a knife blade and holds on. And I suddenly realize why. I should have felt guilt, but I didn't.

"I—I'm sorry," I mutter through clenched teeth. Only then does the pain let up.

A smile hints at the corners of Mary Margaret's wrinkled mouth. "Are you all right?"

I nod. I am.

"All right," says Mary Margaret. She steps back, allowing me space to get up. I glance around the sick room, noticing the gray faces staring at me like I'm some freak.

"What are you all staring at?" I shout.

When they finally look away, I glare at Mary Margaret. Her smile has disappeared.

"Do you know where you are?" she says.

I shrug. Like I care.

"This is a *hospice*, Kip. A place where people come to die." She sighs and her face doesn't look so angry now. She motions toward a bed the woman in scrubs is straightening. "Mrs. Brandt passed early this morning and we were here to help her through it. I'll put up with your sneers and your irreverence everywhere but in this room. One word from me to Carmen Slater and you'll be back in prison, Kip—artificial conscience or not. Is that clear?"

I'm not sure what she means by irreverence, but I nod.

"All right then. I think you've seen enough for the day. I'll show you to your room and let you get settled. We'll start over tomorrow when you've gotten a little of the vinegar out of your system.

It feels weird having so much room to myself. I'm not used to spending the night in such a frilly, big room. The four-poster bed with its lace bows, all pink and sugary-sweet. It's enough to make me puke. I crawl out of the bed, my tracking anklet bulky and heavy as I stumble into the bathroom. If they can put this thing in my head to teach me how to act, why can't they do the same thing with this lousy anklet? Maybe it's because they don't want me to forget why I'm here and what I've done?

I scowl at the mirror. My mousy hair needs washing. I look at how much thinner I am than I was five years ago when they carted me off to prison. I'm not sure I know the person staring back at me, but I'm not sure I knew her any better five years ago.

After I stand around in the shower for a while, not having to watch my back for once, I towel dry my hair, dress, and wander into the hallway. I eventually find my way back to the foyer where Mary Margaret stands looking tense.

"I was afraid you'd drowned down there."

"Hey, that's the first real shower I've seen in years. Give me a break."

Mary Margaret turns away and in a tired voice, she tells me to come with her. Time to run the maze. I follow. Where else am I going to go?

Down the hall again and we're in that huge bunkroom with its marble tabletops and comforters and sick people. The smell of old piss and bleach gags me. Old Mary Margaret whirls and shakes a finger at me.

"You remember what I told you yesterday, Kip. You'll show respect in this room."

I nod slowly. A lot of them are just old people past their time. I walk down the aisle, trying to pretend they aren't here with their wheezing and moaning.

I say, "It's kinda funny, don't you think? I helped Donny kill a guy and now, my community service is to help people die. I wasn't trying to be irrelevant or whatever."

Mary Margaret laughs. "Irreverent, Kip. Not irrelevant."

"Whatever," I say. "So how do I figure into this experiment?" I have to ask someone and Mary Margaret seems like she tells it straight. Not like Carmen. She just tells me what I want to hear.

"They want to test your implant in this environment. See if it gives you compassion."

"That's it?" I ask. How lame.

"No," she answers, her voice tired. "Kip, do you believe in the soul?"

I shrug.

"No one has proven it one way or another," she says. Her eyes seem to light up now, like she's really into this stuff. "Some University of Washington researchers are trying to answer that question. They're trying to measure the existence of the soul."

I smile. "I'd make a good test case. The judge said I didn't have one."

Mary Margaret laughs again. "They're only studying terminally ill patients, Kip." She points at two women in white scrubs standing at the end of a bed. The red-haired one's messing with a box on a table and the dark-haired one is typing stuff on a datapad. "They're measuring brain chemicals before and after death."

"Yeah, right. And whose dumb-assed idea was that?"

She straightens her back and I can tell I've made her mad again.

"It was mine."

I let the words settle for a moment. Not sure what I should say, but a pain in my stomach reminds me that maybe I've hurt her feelings.

"Sorry," I mutter. Just feels right somehow to say that. "Why'd you want to do this?"

"I'm getting old," she says with a sigh. Her voice is quieter now. The anger's going away. "I'd like to know where we go from here."

I've thought about that some, when the prosecutor asked for the death penalty for Donny. I don't know what's out there. Donny says there's nothing, just emptiness, but it makes me wonder sometimes. Especially when I look at the night sky and the ocean. Just feels like there should be more to it. Maybe that's why Donny likes to walk on the beach and stand at the edge of the water? Because, for a little while, it lets him wonder.

"You think there's something beyond here?" I ask, trying my best not to sound bitchy.

She smiles. "Yes, there has to be. Look at the mountains and the forests. There's order and reason to it, and we place our trust in that."

So many times I've wanted to believe things weren't just all out of control and everything. Like that night in the alley. It seems to hang in my thoughts more and more now.

"Your first assignment is to fill all the pitchers with water. When you're finished with that, there's laundry to fold and beds to make."

I do what she asks. I fill all the pitchers. Takes me a half hour, but I manage. When I'm finished, I find her sitting with a white-haired woman, whose face is all wrinkled and pasty.

"I'm done with the pitchers," I say. "Do you want me to start on the laundry?"

"Sit," she says, like I'm her dog.

"Why should I?"

"Because I asked you. Please."

I don't feel like arguing, so I sit.

"Kip, this is Mrs. Sanderson. She's eighty-three."

I stare blankly into the woman's pale green eyes.

"Hello, Kip," she says in a raspy voice. She smiles. "Thank you for sitting with me a bit."

I frown. Like it's my idea.

Old Mary Margaret nudges me with her shoe. Damn, she's expecting me to actually talk to this woman. "Uh, sure."

"You remind me of my granddaughter," chirps the woman, a smile still on her face. Her eyes get all dreamy and wet. "Sarah was such a sweet girl."

"What happened to her?" I ask. My little sister's name is Sarah, but when Mom split, she took Sarah with her. Left me with my dad who spent more time stinking drunk than anything. He drank himself to death at forty-three. Sometimes though, through his booze stupors, he'd cry for Mom. I stopped crying for both of them a long time ago.

"Sarah died last year in a car accident. She was fourteen. Like you, she had her whole life ahead of her."

I start to laugh, but my gut feels all quivery and sick. I look away, thinking of my sister and realize it would be good to see her again. She lives in Idaho with Mom. I get a crazy idea that I should go see her. She's the only person who's ever cared about me.

I look at the old woman, who's still smiling, and my gut aches again.

"I'm sorry," I whisper, not sure where the words are coming from. "My sister's name is Sarah. She's sixteen now."

To my surprise, the old woman reaches out with claw-like, twisted hands and pats my arm.

I let her touch me. Her fingers are cold and rough and my first instinct is to pull away, but I force it down. I'm surprised that we have something in common. God, that's strange.

"Mrs. Sanderson is part of the test," says Mary Margaret. She points to the box sitting beside the water pitchers. It's about the size of an alarm clock. A red-haired woman, one of ones in scrubs, walks to the box and records some numbers.

"Bev, this is Kip, my new—" Mary Margaret looks at me for a moment and doesn't say anything.

"Felon," I say.

Mary Margaret's face twitches. "Kip, that's not what I—"

"It's okay," I say. "I know what I am."

For a few moments, no one says a word, but then the red-haired woman, Bev, turns toward me. "Kip, these monitors are recording data from each patient, so it's very important that they are working properly at all times."

I frown. "So you want me to check the boxes? Make sure they're all still working?"

Bev smiles, but it's not like Carmen's fake smile. "Exactly. When we have a complete set of data, we're going to compare the levels at time of death for any changes. And maybe identify some part of the soul."

"But why do you bother?" I ask. Who cares if it exists or not?

"The soul is our essence, Kip. When everything else breaks down, our soul is who we are inside. If we can prove it exists, then maybe death won't be so scary."

I've never thought about death being scary before. "How will you know if anything changes?"

"A good question," says Bev. She taps a small light on the front of the box. "If the numbers fluctuate significantly at time of death, then this indicator will flash. It may not prove anything, but the difference will be worth investigating."

The weeks slip into months and I find that these stiffs aren't the pains in the ass I thought they'd be. Nobody whines or complains much, but in their faces I see pain. Bev talks to me sometimes, asking me if I've had any trouble with the boxes.

Mary Margaret has had me eating lunch with her for weeks now. She's really not so bad. She tells good stories. And she's made me sit with Mrs. Sanderson every day. She's not so bad either.

"Sarah loved to play sports," says Mrs. Sanderson, her hand on mine. "Especially soccer. Do you play sports?"

"None that are legal."

Mrs. Sanderson laughs and for a moment the shadows on her face fade a little. I can almost see what she was like before she came here, but when the gray returns, I know she's dying. She looks past me now. I glance over my shoulder, but nobody's there.

"I'm not going to be here long," she says suddenly.

My throat tightens. "Why do you say that?" I don't like to hear her say that.

"I've seen her a few times—my Sarah. Once in the middle of the night. Yesterday, by the window." Her gaze is so far away. "And just now, behind you. My husband, Harry, too. I'm not scared. I'm ready to go. They're waiting for me."

I think of her Sarah, then I can't help but think of that guy—the one Donny killed. The events of that night in the alley come rushing back to me. Pounding through my brain in still life, frame-by-frame images. Almost like I can stop it. Almost.

Donny holds the gun and I'm rifling through the guy's pockets. He's tall and dark, his suit expensive. "Don't make me kill you, man," Donny growls, his face all wild and flushed. "Just give me the money." Freeze-frame.

The wallet's in my hands now, soft black leather smelling old and kind of like cedar. The money's crisp and stiff. Creased pictures hide behind the bills. His dark eyes hold mine in an unnatural stare and I smell his sour fear. He trembles beneath his black overcoat. His gaze flicks from Donny, to the gun, to me and I start to laugh. His fear makes me feel important. Someone's giving me their undivided attention.

I hold out the wallet to him, displaying my prize, daring him to challenge me. Freeze-frame.

The words hang hollow in my ears. "Please," the man's voice quivers. "Take the money, just don't kill me!"

I laugh and run my hand down Donny's arm. I feel drunk—delirious. I like the echo of my voice in the alley. I like that I hold all the cards. Freeze-frame.

The gun barrel shadows in the glint of light from an overhead window as Donny raises the gun from his hip. It's sleek and black. Donny grins.

The guy's nostrils flare. His eyes widen. His whole body winds tight, his hands out, fingers spreading. His lips purse, a raw, desperate noise escaping.

Donny leers at the guy. He licks his lips, his eyes hungry.

Pop! God, the noise sounds so fake. Like a kid's toy. The guy jerks backward, his body flailing against the wall as his back comes apart. It all moves so slow, so surreal. Blood hits my cheek. I want to kick him. The dumb-ass made Donny shoot him. I stand there staring at him as he slides down the wall in a smear of blood. I want to scream and shake him.

Tears track down my face, the ache in my gut burning and throbbing. I double over, feeling so sick. It all seems so unreal now and all I can think about is that wallet. I never even looked at those pictures, but I think about them now. I wonder what he left behind that night. What we took from him that night. I shudder, thinking of my folks and Sarah. Mrs. Sanderson and her granddaughter.

And for the first time, I feel bad. I feel so bad. It was our fault. I know that now and it makes me gag. What if it had been this old lady? Or Mary Margaret?

Mrs. Sanderson's hand is still on mine. Mary Margaret is staring at me, saying nothing.

"Are you all right, Kip?" she asks finally, quietly.

I can't speak and I don't want them to see me cry, but dammit, I just can't help myself. I shake my head and rise from the bed, my arms folded against my stomach, and I run toward the bathroom.

Dry heaves rip through my gut. I drop down in front of a toilet. Again and again, I wretch air, but the sickness lies in my stomach like a rock. No matter what, I can't get rid of it.

Hands touch my shoulders and I jump, starting to pull away, but a voice fills my ears.

"You're okay," says Mary Margaret in a soft voice. "They told me this would be the hard part of your service. It'll get better. Facing our mistakes is hard, but you'll get through it."

I wretch again, but I don't try to pull away from her. Finally, my stomach settles and I lean against the wall. Mary Margaret kneels beside me, studying my face as she waits for me to say something. For a long time, I can only stare at her.

"I've seen that night a lot of times in my head," I say, "but not like I did today."

She squints at me. "What was different?"

I bite my lip. "This time, I cared." My throat feels tight again and my voice thins. "That guy in the alley. We just killed him like he was nothing. Like it didn't matter." I suck in a breath of air, thinking again of Mrs. Sanderson's Sarah—my sister, Sarah. "Like he didn't matter."

"It will be bad for a while, but then the pain will start to fade."

I frown. "How do you know?"

"Because we all have guilt, Kip. A little bit is healthy. Keeps us humble."

It's all new to me. I can only shrug.

"C'mon," Mary Margaret says with a grunt and rises to her feet. "Let's go check on some of the other residents."

Slowly, I get to my feet and I follow her into the bunkroom. She looks a bit thinner in the waist. She puts an arm around my shoulder and I remember a time when Mom use to do that. Mary Margaret isn't so bad.

I've been checking the boxes for a few weeks now, the rush of numbers and quiet little beeps confusing. I've never dealt with something like this before, but I do my work. I fill all the pitchers and straighten the beds. Mary Margaret hasn't been around much lately, always locking herself away in her office to deal with paperwork. I'd never admit it, but I miss her being around. Carmen's come to check up on me twice now, spending a lot of time with Mary Margaret. Every time I see her, my hackles raise. I wonder what

Mary Margaret's telling her about me. Part of me doesn't care, but sometimes, I think about it and I get mad.

Mrs. Sanderson kicked off three weeks ago and that stupid box didn't show anything different. Mary Margaret says that nothing changed. She doesn't seem too bummed over the results. She's more upset over losing Mrs. Sanderson. But I'm not. Mrs. Sanderson wanted to go. She'd told me that nearly every day, that she was ready, but Mary Margaret cries a lot and seems real messed up by the whole thing. I try to tell her Mrs. Sanderson was okay with it, but she doesn't want to listen. She calls me callous and tells me to fill the water pitchers. I swear, with all this pitcher filling, I'm going to drown these people before my CS is over.

When I finish, I wander out of the bunk room. Light from Mary Margaret's door shines into the dim hallway ahead and I move toward it. The door is part-way open, but I hesitate, trying to gather my words and hoping I don't say something stupid.

"Mary Margaret," I say finally and poke my head into the room.

It's dark except for the scalding desk light. She sits there unmoving with her head in her hands.

"What is it, Kip?" she asks, her voice weary. "I'm not in the mood for your antics today." Her face looks thin.

"I just wanted to tell you I'm sorry you miss Mrs. Sanderson so much. She wanted to go, you know. She said it's cool because she has people waiting for her."

Mary Margaret wipes her eyes with her hand and stares at me for a moment. Finally, she smiles. "Thank you, Kip."

I nod, feeling uncomfortable again, and start to slip out of the room, but she calls me back.

"It isn't just losing Mrs. Sanderson that I'm crying about," she says, her voice steady.

"Is it the experiment?"

Mary Margaret shakes her head slow and there's something in her eyes that sends a jolt of fear through me. Like she's given up or something. That look scares me. I saw it in that guy in the alley.

"No, I'm just being selfish, I guess. See, Mrs. Sanderson had cancer." Tears drip down her wrinkled face. "And so do I. They gave me six months and I've been around a year now. My luck's about run out, too, Kip." She sighs. "I wanted to be here, to help you through your service."

Damn her! I want to slap her face. Just another one-way ticket. "It doesn't matter," I say in the calmest voice I can manage. Damn Mary Margaret for making me like her. "I don't need anybody's help."

"Anybody? No. You need somebody. Somebody who can reach you and so far, I'm it, kid."

"They'll just send me someplace else," I say. "I'll be okay, like always." She's leaving me—like everybody else. I turn toward the door, hiding my face from her. If I look at her I'm going to cry and then she'll know how much I care.

"I care what happens to you, Kip. We're making progress and I don't want it to stop." Her voice sounds so warm and concerned. I choke up, my throat hot and aching.

I drop down in the chair and fight against the sting in my eyes. "I don't care, do you hear?" I cross my arms and chant the phrase over and over to myself, but the tears slip down my face. Damned rehab.

She moves around the desk, her breathing heavy, and puts her hand on my arm. I jerk away.

"I trusted you!" I shout, my voice raw. I glare at her, but my bottom lip begins to quiver. I sink into the chair. "I don't want you to die," I say, the tears choking me.

Her eyes are watery as she puts her arms around me. My shoulders heave and everything spews. I can't hold it back. I tell her about my mom and Sarah and how I don't care about anyone, but she just holds me. Maybe she doesn't believe me?

"I'm not making this up," I say.

"I know," says Mary Margaret, her voice steady. "I'm just glad you're trusting me with the story. I do care, Kip. Please believe me. I care what happens to you."

Silence is all I can respond with. No one's ever said that to me before. "See, I'm going to need your help very soon," she says. "You'll need to check all the monitors thoroughly, including mine. It's important to me, especially now. Promise you'll take care of this for me."

With a nod, I rise from the chair and excuse myself. I feel sicker than I have since my rehab session.

Two more people die over the next couple of weeks, but Bev's boxes don't seem to record any differences . Each time, Mary Margaret gets all depressed and quiet. Finally, one morning, I'm filling pitchers when Bev taps me on the shoulder, startling me.

"Kip?" she says, her eyes wide and her face pale.

"What is it?" I ask.

"Mary Margaret's ill," she says, her voice quiet.

All the air rushes out of my lungs. I try to take a deep breath and pretend like I don't care, but I can't do that anymore. Damn this thing in my head! I count the seconds to myself and try to hold it all together.

"Where is she?" I ask finally.

Bev points to the doorway. Mary Margaret's slumped there, one of the hospice workers and some of the researchers hanging over her. Just standing there gawking and not doing a damn thing to help. I hurry across the room and shove through them.

"Either help or get out of the way!" I shout. They move.

I force a smile to my lips as I bend down to Mary Margaret. "Hey, why you laying around when there's so much stuff to get done?" I ask.

She returns my smile, but she's so weak, so thin. "Kip, I need your help."

"You need somebody's wallet ganked?"

A thin laugh slips through her teeth as I put my arms around her waist and haul her to her feet. I keep my arm around her as we walk toward the empty bed near the bathroom. There's a window across from the bed at least, so she can see outside. I've known for a while that Mary Margaret would end up here. It's an awful long walk and I wish we weren't making it. My gut feels quivery and hurts, a different sort of hurt this time. An empty feeling. God, it hurts.

I help her under the covers. Then I drop down beside the bed, feeling stupid, but part of me doesn't care anymore.

"Kip," she answers, her voice wheezy and thin. "Check my monitor. Want to—make sure it's working."

I fumble behind the thing and press a test button. It lights green. "It's fine. What happened?"

"I'm not feeling well. Started late last night. I'm not going to be here long."

How does she know that? How did Mrs. Sanderson know? I swallow hard. Did that guy in the alley know?

"I'm scared, Kip."

My eyes sting. I reach out and put my hand on hers, squeezing. "It's okay," I tell her. "Mrs. Sanderson saw all those people waiting for her, remember. There's got to be a regular crowd waiting for you. Isn't that better than one of those dumb ol' boxes flashing at you?"

Her eyes get all weepy and her voice sort of chokes out. She nods.

My gut aches so bad and my hands tremble. It's all so much harder when you care, but I'm no coward. She's done it for all these people. I'll do it for her. "I'll stay with you as long as you want me."

"I'd like that," she says. Her face is droopy and gray, like Mrs. Sanderson before she died. I feel so scared, but I'm not going to leave her now. I've got to let her know that I'm her friend and that I'm glad for everything she's done for me.

"See, besides Donny, I've never had a friend. They tell me Donny's not my friend, but he's all I've ever known." I force myself to smile. "Now, I got comparisons." My throat tightens, my eyes burning, and I can barely talk. "Thank you, Mary Margaret."

"Thank you, Kelly," she says and I choke up. Mom used to call me Kelly when I was little. I became Kip when she took Sarah and moved away. I wipe back tears from my eyes.

"I'm not religious and I don't know about souls or what happens when we die," I say, my voice all shaky now, "but if you see that guy—the one in the alley . . . that we killed . . . would you tell him I'm sorry? Really sorry?"

She nods. "You're going to be all right."

The hours pass and the grayness hugging the edges of her face spreads. Her eyes look weak and her breathing's so shallow. Outside, the grayness settles around the place, like everything will just blot her out and she'll fade away. My hand is still holding hers, but it's been some time since she's squeezed it. I glance over at the box. What will it record? Will that light flash when she dies?

Bev walks over and adjusts some sort of monitor attached to Mary Margaret's temple and another attached to her chest. She pats me on the shoulder and walks away.

Toward afternoon, Mary Margaret begins to mumble, but I can't tell what she's saying. Even if I lean down, the words are too soft. I wonder what she's going on about, but I'll never know, I realize.

As afternoon slips away, so does Mary Margaret. Her chest rattles. It's a hollow sort of damp sound. Her breathing's fading. I rise from my chair, but I hold onto her hand. With her other hand, she reaches up at something I can't see. Slowly, the rise and fall of her chest lessens until finally, it just stops.

I glance at the box on the table beside the bed. Nothing. No flash, no light. Only a soft hum comes from the other monitor.

I let go of her hand and stand in front of the window, my knees shaky. Behind me, I hear feet pounding across the room. A faint alarm sounds from the flat-lined monitor. I try to tune it out. Two women in scrubs huddle beside Mary Margaret as they try to revive her.

I stare at the intense blue-green of the Pacific Ocean against the rocky shore. They won't be bringing Mary Margaret back. She's cast her soul to the sea.

Maybe, just about that, Donny is right? I think I understand his words now. And Bev's, too.

Over the ocean, thick, gray clouds part and sunlight pours down on the water. The light is almost white, the flickering so bright I squint and my eyes burn. Then it fades into the grayness again. I glance at the box. Dark. Silent.

I don't need that box to flash or anything else right now. All I need now is time. And when it feels right, there's a trip I need to take. I'd like to tell Sarah about the mistakes I've made. But most of all, I'd like to tell her about Mary Margaret and this place—Mary Margaret's spirit house. At least, this is where I found mine.

CIRCLE OF LIFE

The chi is spongy in my hands and it's difficult to mold. I've never done this before, but I know that with practice, I'll learn.

In the darkness, I touch my own face, feeling only remembrance. The memory of the roundness of lips, curve of cheek and chin, and gentle slope of nose. I want something better than that imperfect form. Deep in memory, I recall a phrase that had once been so important to me. Now, it only serves as a sliver of guidance in the void. Leave things better than you find them.

With measured strokes, I shape the chi, molding it tall and straight, graceful. It is difficult to work without seeing, but memory is what I must work from. My patience makes the resistant chi turn pliable, at last becoming torso, arms then legs. Running my fingers over the soft material, I carefully smooth it.

The hands I mold stronger, the fingers more slender and dexterous. They must hold more than I ever dreamed they could. Molding, smoothing, stretching, the fingers take shape on each hand. Five—it's familiar. These digits are in the image of my own, only more supple and flexible. Expressing more care and comfort than my own mortal hands ever could. I balance the legs with feet, concentrating on fluidity of motion. On endurance. Male or female? I decide on both.

I don't know how long I've been refining and shaping. It feels an eternity, but I'm beyond the human construct of time now. That is something else I must create, but not just yet. There is so much to do and it can't be rushed, especially since I'm still learning.

Once more, I run my hands over the chi's inanimate shape, leveling, sculpting until I am satisfied with the form. The chi is very old. I am amazed this ageless life essence can be molded yet one more time. Only then do I allow the stars to light the void and illuminate the eyes. The view is infinite and will give the eyes vision.

When my world's sun went dark and earth turned cold and empty, my last breaths were spent in apprehension. Was there anything beyond this cold and pain? Would I cease to exist or would my soul journey? If so—to where?

Touching the cold brow, I infuse it with memories of before, of the only world I ever knew. Earth, the place from which I evolved. A place I hold dear. Only through this form can I touch and feel the simplicity of being human again. Before, the day-to-day tasks of living seemed so complicated, so narrowly focused and self-absorbed. How little I understood. How constrained I felt. What I did, I did for myself. What didn't directly affect me, I ignored.

For all my trepidations, I am beyond those mortal constraints now. My world has become the universe and with a thought, I can be everywhere and anywhere. But with that freedom comes the responsibility for a new humanity, my next challenge.

I'm careful not to transfer the flaws and there are so many. I filter away the biases and fear. But I am so limited by my origins. I feel so small and insignificant compared to my own creator, so afraid of failing. How can I stand in those shoes? Maybe with practice, creation will get easier?

Within this body, I balance sun with moon, light with dark, day with night, reason with emotion. Yin with yang. On the hands, I sprinkle diamonds for strength, patience, and gentleness. On the feet, I scatter oak leaves for endurance. The heart I cleanse with rainwater before I encircle it with flame. What can't be cleansed will be tempered. Tempering mortal nature, it is something I remember lacking. What I didn't understand, I feared. What I didn't like, I hated. What I believed was the truth. I won't allow those flaws to be passed on again. It is difficult to impart this newfound wisdom, so I rely on symbols of life before. It's all I know right now.

The last question haunts me, my uncertainty growing. I'm alone to complete this task just as the others from my world have evolved to similar tasks. It's the next step to understanding myself and my world that has fallen away. Free will? Do I pass that on or do I withhold it?

How would I have learned without my own human mistakes—as painful as they were—to guide me? When I touched fire, I learned to be careful. When I heard music, I learned about preference. When I tasted wine, I learned about craving.

In the end, I know there is only one answer. When it is their time to become as me, they will remember and maybe they will leave things better than they find them, too? So the circle of life continues.

One last time, I burnish and refine the chi form. At last, it is ready. My first prototype. My plan is all laid out and when I create time, it will slowly reveal itself. But so much can—and will—go wrong. And if so, I know I cannot intervene because I have passed on free will. I'm not sure I'm prepared for those moments, but that's part of my learning, too.

I imagine the world I have already created. I blink and it is before me. Newborn blue and green sphere with oceans and forests and mountains. Warm sunlight from a star I've never seen touches its surface, so far from the old world. This place is empty of life, but now, I will change that.

The breath of life fills my lungs, but I pause. Have I learned enough to take this first step of creation? I have stood in their shoes and I have survived mortality. Maybe this understanding will lead me to knowledge?

With a deep breath, I exhale life into the prototype as I gently place it on the new world. Its chest expands as lungs fill with the first mortal breath. The chi now resonates with a spirit that will find its way back to me.

From this prototype, I will make copies and variations. And I will watch my plan unfold as my new world fills the void. To deepen my understanding and learn about the universe, I must first be its creator. And there was evening and there was morning—a new world, a new day.

PUBLICATION HISTORY

"When the Sparrow Falls," first appeared in *Cemetery Sonata*, ed. June Hubbard, Chameleon Publishing, April 1999.

"The Sound of Angels," first appeared in *Bending the Landscape: Fantasy*, ed. Nicola Griffith & Steve Pagel, White Wolf, 1997.

"Midnight Oil," *100 Wicked Little Witch Stories*, ed. Stefan Dziemianowicz, Robert Weinberg & Martin H. Greenberg, Barnes & Noble, 1995.

"Wild Feed," is original to this collection.

"Homecoming," first appeared in *The Age of Reason*, ed. Kurt Roth, SFF Net, 1999

"A Universal Spectrum," is original to this collection.

"Peace of Lace," first appeared in *Sirius Visions*, August 1, 1994.

"Surviving the Elephant," first appeared in *Civil War Fantastic*, ed. Martin H. Greenberg, DAW, 2000.

"Central Premise," first appeared in *Galaxy*, Jul/Aug 1994.

"Snow Angels," first appeared in *Millenium SF & F*, March 1997

"Rena 733," first appeared in *Treachery and Treason*, ed. Laura Anne Gilman & Jennifer Heddle, Roc, 2000.

"The Mermaid's Looking Glass," is original to this collection.

"Nightweaver," first appeared in *Blood Muse*, ed. Esther M. Friesner & Martin H. Greenberg, Fine, 1995.

"Whispers," first appeared in *Hauntings*, ed. L. Marie Wood, Cyber-Pulp, March 2004.

"Safe As the Dark," first appeared in *switch.blade: School's Out*, ed. by Amy Sterling Casil, July 2002.

"The Essence of Place," first appeared in *Age of Wonders*, ed. Jeffry Dwight, SFF Net, 2000.

"Music to Her Ears," first appeared in *Prom Night*, ed. Nancy Springer, DAW, 1999.

"The Spirit House," first appeared in *Quantum Speculative Fiction*, November 1999.

"Circle of Life," first appeared in *Beyond the Last Star*, ed. Sherwood Smith, SFF Net, 2002